PERSUADED

and

Rescued

THE HEIR'S LADY IN SHINING ARMOUR

BY
BREE WOLF

Persuaded & Rescued - The Heir's Lady in Shining Armour
by Bree Wolf

This is a work of fiction. Names, characters, businesses, places, brands, media, events and incidents are either the products of the author's imagination or used in a fictitious manner.

Any resemblance to actual persons, living or dead, or actual events is purely coincidental.

Copyright © 2020 Sabrina Wolf
Papaerback ISBN: 978-3-96482-064-8
Hardcover ISBN: 978-3-96482-123-2

www.breewolf.com

To my son's new school
For giving him a home away from home

Acknowledgments

This story would never have seen the light of day if I had not been able to stop worrying. And I finally did stop worrying because we found the perfect school for my son after all. He is happy there. He feels cherished and respected, cared for and treasured. He can be who he is, is allowed the time and space to discover the world without pressure and censure and reproach and wakes every morning, happy that it is a school day.

Thank you "AMSEL-Schule" (Blackbird School)! No words can ever do justice to what you have done for us. To always remember this moment, I asked my cover designer to add a little blackbird to the cover of this novella.

My dearest thanks also go to my wonderful readers. My devoted team of beat readers perused the manuscript and offered their advice, their criticism as well as their applause. I tweaked the story here and there, exterminated the occasional — or not so occasional — typo and found myself reading through a story that was much more well-rounded. Thank you so much!

PERSUADED and Rescued

Prologue

London, England, spring 1798 (or a variation thereof)

Miss Maryann Hayes felt a cold shiver crawl down her back as her father bade her to sit down. His gaze barely met hers, and his grey hair looked oddly tousled as though he had been running his hands through it again and again. Deep lines furrowed his forehead, and the corners of his mouth, drooped downward, a far cry from the kind smile she had often seen upon his face.

"Is everything all right, Father?" Maryann's voice shook as her gaze drifted from her father's to her mother's. In all her years, Maryann had never seen her parents so distraught. Something had to be very wrong.

Her father inhaled a deep breath, once more ran his hand shakily through his hair and then turned pleading eyes to his wife.

For a brief moment, Maryann's mother closed her eyes before her shoulders drew back, and she sat down next to her daughter on the settee. Her hands reached out to grasp Maryann's, pulling them gently into her own. "You are quite right to be concerned, my dear," her mother began, never having been one to pretend the truth was anything less than what it was. "You might have suspected that our financial situation has been most dire these past few years." She glanced up at her husband, who turned away and walked toward the window, his gaze fixed outside on something else. "Although your father has worked most diligently on repaying your uncle's debts, I am afraid that it simply was not enough." Her mother heaved a deep sigh, and a touch of disapproval came to her pale blue eyes at the memory of her brother-in-law.

Maryann felt her hands tense in her mother's, relieved to not be alone in this situation. Always had she known that her father's elder brother had been nothing more than a drunkard. Her parents had done their utmost to hide the sad truth from her; however, Maryann had always been a most observant child, and her uncle had been most obvious in the way he had lived his life. As the eldest, he had inherited title and estate; however, it had been his younger brother who had seen to everything, who had shouldered the responsibility, but who had not been able to prevent his brother from wasting their funds on drink and frivolities.

Maryann nodded. "I know you did your best," she said, looking up at her father's turned back, knowing how much it hurt him to not be able to give her a dowry. Often had she heard her parents discuss this particular matter, their regret only too visible on their distraught faces. "I assure you, I do not wish for a dowry," she promised him as much as herself. "I do not care for pretty things and silly trappings. All I care for is finding a man who looks at me as you look at Mother."

She felt her mother's hands give hers a gentle squeeze, and her eyes turned to the woman who had taken care of her her entire life. "I'm so very sorry, my dear," her mother choked out, her eyes glistening with tears. "Unfortunately, it is much worse."

Maryann tensed. "Worse?" Once again, her gaze drifted from her mother to her father and back again. "What do you mean?"

Her mother inhaled a fortifying breath. "Our funds are all but depleted," she admitted with an anguished look upon her face. "Before long, we will have to sell this house as well as everything else that is not entailed. We will not be able to maintain many in our employ, if any at all." She swallowed hard, her gaze flitting to her husband before returning to her daughter. "Debtors will still be knocking on our door until the end of our days. That is the sad truth, one we can no longer shield you from, my dear."

Shocked into stillness, Maryann glanced at her father, his shoulders slumped, and his head bowed in defeat. It broke her heart to see him thus, and she knew in that moment that she would do everything within her power to lift his burden, to carry her share, to see him smile again. "I know you cannot provide me with a dowry," she whispered into the stillness of the room, "but perhaps there is still a way for me to make a good match. Perhaps before our situation becomes known, I will be able to find a suitor who would be willing to marry me and save our family from ruin."

At her words, her father slowly turned from the window, his gaze tense as it fell upon her. "No, my dear, this is not your burden to bear. I will not have you sacrifice your happiness to right something that was not your doing."

Maryann loved her father for his objection, but it made her all the more determined. "But I wish to marry," Maryann insisted, knowing she must not show any insecurity, or her parents would never allow her. She rose to her feet, pulling her mother along with her. "I wish for a husband, a family and children. Why should I not find that which I wish for with a man who can also provide us with the funds we need? It might not be...highly likely, but it is not impossible, either."

A warm smile came to mother's face as she patted Maryann's hand. "You have the kindest of hearts, my dear." She sighed and glanced at her husband. "Indeed, should you find such a man, we would not object; however, we do not wish for you to enter into a marriage that will not bring you happiness."

"All my life," Maryann told her parents with affection, "I have dreamed of a match such as yours. However, as a woman grown, I do know that marriage and love do not always walk hand in hand. Even without debtors knocking on our door, I might never cross paths with the man who would own my heart. But does that mean I'll have to remain unwed forever? Would it not be preferable to choose a match, a man I can respect, who is kind and devoted, who will give me the family I long to have?"

Her mother sighed, and a meaningful look passed between her

parents. "You must choose your own path," her mother told her kindly; still, a warning reverberated in her voice, "But do not forget that a path once chosen cannot be unchosen. The man you choose today, you will have to live with for the rest of your life. I will not tell you what to do, but I cannot help but encourage you to not only rely upon your mind when making this particular choice."

Maryann nodded, once more squeezing her mother's hands. "I thank you for your concern. It warms my heart." She turned to smile at her father. "I assure you I will do as you say. I will choose wisely and allow my heart to guide me." Looking at her parents, seeing the love they held for her, Maryanne knew that with or without love, she would find a suitor, who could see beyond her lack of dowry and offer his assistance. Never had she lost her heart to anyone, and often had she wondered if she ever would. Perhaps it had been a blessing in disguise, for now it allowed her to choose without thought for how her heart might survive if she had to relinquish a love most dear to her. Many marriages started without love. They were born out of convenience, out of something mutually beneficial to both parties; however, over time, love and affection might still develop. Perhaps that was the path meant for her. Perhaps she simply had to be patient.

"In fact," Maryann stated, trying to make her voice sound as enthusiastic and positive as she possibly could, "I already have a gentleman in mind." She looked from her father to her mother, seeing their surprise. "He has asked me to dance once or twice and spoken kindly to me."

Her father's mouth opened, and she could see he was ready to object. However, Maryann rushed on before he could. "I'm not saying I will marry him. All I'm saying is that he is a kind man, and that I will try to get to know him better." She smiled at her father. "Surely, there is no harm in that, is there?"

The corners of his mouth twitched as he walked toward her, the ghost of his usual smile teasing his lips. His warm hands sought one of hers, holding on tightly as he looked at her. "Of course, my dear, there is no harm in that; however, I know your devoted heart, and I would urge you to consider your next steps wisely, for I can see that your mind has already formed a plan." The hint of a teasing smirk appeared on his weathered face. "Do you deny it?"

Maryann chuckled, cherishing the sound as well as the feeling it brought to her chest. "You know me too well, Father." She straightened and pulled back her shoulders, her chin lifting. "Please, trust me. You've always allowed me to choose my own path. I promise I shall not disappoint you now."

Her mother brushed a hand over Maryann's cheek. "It is not our disappointment we fear, but yours. But you are right, my dear. You are a woman grown, and we have never known you to make rash, unwise decisions." Another meaningful look passed between her parents. "We will trust you as we always have. We only urge you to continue on the same path as before and not veer from it."

"I promise," Maryann said, uncertain if she was speaking the truth in that moment. Certainly, marrying the wrong man for the wrong reasons would lead to unhappiness; however, seeing her parents reduced to the direst of circumstances would also break her heart. It was a dilemma she had never thought she would find herself in, but here it was, and a choice needed to be made.

Perhaps Fortune would smile upon her though and guide her in the right direction, bringing her path to cross that of someone she could lose her heart to after all.

Chapter One

GUILT OF THE FORTUNATE

London, England

Five months later

"Why the long face?" The Marquess of Elmridge asked his eldest son. "I'm not dead yet. The responsibility is not yet yours. Why do you look so aggrieved?" An amused chuckle rumbled in his father's throat, his brown eyes twinkling with mirth as he looked upon Leopold.

"William!" his mother chided with a disapproving look as she strode forward and gave her husband a slight slap upon the shoulder. "That is certainly nothing to be jesting about. I will not have you talk of such things; do you hear me?" She gave her husband a stern look; still, it could not hide the fear that lingered, a fear that spoke of one dreading the day when one would lose another who was most beloved.

Aside from winking at his wife, the marquess ignored her disapproval, his gaze returning to fix upon his son.

Leopold rolled his eyes at his father, then slumped down in one of the chairs opposite his desk. "I'm not aggrieved, I assure you, dear

7

Father. I'm merely..." Indeed, what was he? That was the question, was it not?

"Yes?" his father prompted, gently patting his wife's hand which had come to rest upon his shoulder. She stood beside him as he sat behind his large desk, an image of companionship, walking hand-in-hand, one leaning on the other. Always had they seemed as one, certain in who they were, together and alone. Always had Leopold envied them that certainty.

Leopold sighed, "I'm not certain I can explain," he admitted, bowing his head as though he had failed his father. "I see all you do every day, and I wonder how I will ever manage." Indeed, what he had said was not wrong; however, it was not the whole truth.

The truth was that Leopold did not know who he was, what kind of man. Was he like his father? Like both his parents? Would he find fulfilment in tending to his estate and the people dependent upon him? Did he possess the necessary wisdom, patience and determination needed to attend to everything under his care? He knew what his duty was, and he would never shirk it. But sometimes, in the dark of night and the brightness of day, he worried and wondered and wished he could be certain that his path would not only be one of duty and responsibility, but also be one that would eventually bring him happiness.

He did not simply wish to be the heir.

He also wanted to be simply Leopold.

His mother's gaze swept over his face, kindness and understanding lingering in her eyes. He saw her squeeze his father's shoulder before she moved away coming to stand behind him, her hands settling upon Leopold's shoulders. "You are young, my dear," she counselled in that soft voice of hers that had always soothed him ever since he had been a little boy. "Live now and do not worry about tomorrow for it will sort itself out, I assure you."

Leopold sighed, knowing that she spoke wisely. Still, the need to be patient riled him. He wanted an answer now, a definitive one, one he could hold to heart, one that would chase away all his doubts. "Do you think," he began tentatively, glancing up at his mother before his gaze moved to his father, "I should marry?"

The question had come rather unexpectedly to him as well; however, Leopold had always dreamed of a marriage like the one his parents had created. To him, they represented closeness and trust and love; they were an ally to one another ~~an ally~~ in the worst of times as well as a friend in the best of times.

His father chuckled, his gaze momentarily lingering upon his wife. "In my opinion, dear son, there is no *should*. You *should* not marry because you believe you have to. You *should* not marry if you do not choose so. There is no *should*." Again, he chuckled, "At least, there *shouldn't* be a *should*."

Leopold found his mother's hands tremble as they rested upon his shoulders. He glanced up and saw her shoulders shaking with silent laughter. "My dear," she said to her husband, "you do have a unique way with words." An affectionate smile came to her face as she shook her head at her husband. Then her gaze moved back to Leopold. "My dear, I believe what your father is trying to say is that duty and responsibility are all well and good, but in the end we need to remember that what makes us happy is rarely rational, rarely born out of duty and responsibility." Her hand slipped from his shoulders, and she crossed the floor once more, coming to stand by her husband's side, one hand settling gently upon his shoulder. For a moment, their eyes met and lingered before she turned and looked back at her son. "If you marry," she told him, the deepest of certainties ringing in her voice, "then let it be for love. It is the only path to true happiness."

Leopold looked at his parents. "How did you know?" He asked as he rose to his feet, his gaze moving from one parent to the other. "How? You knew each other for only a few weeks." He shook his head, dumbfounded. "How did you know?"

To Leopold's displeasure, all his parents did was smile at one another and assure him that he would know when the time came, when he met that one person, he was to share his life with.

Leaving his father's study, Leopold walked into the hall just when the door opened. His good friend Sebastian strode in, his face taut, his shoulders tense. "Hello, there," Leopold greeted him. "I must say, you look about as miserable as I feel myself." He stopped in front of him, shaking his head. "We are a pair, are we not?"

Sebastian chuckled, but it was a dark, defeated sound. "We are indeed. How about a drink?"

Leopold frowned, knowing that his friend often turned to spirits whenever life unsettled him; and a day rarely passed without life unsettling him. "How about a little fresh air?" Leopold offered instead.

Sebastian laughed, a hint of mirth in his eyes. From the dark, gloomy look about him, one would never guess at the humour and kindness that lived in his friend's heart, well hidden beneath disappointment and anger. "You never cease trying, do you?" He stepped closer, his gaze determined as it met Leopold's. "Today we do it my way?"

Leopold sighed, knowing that during the Season his friend frequented his club and similar establishments every night of the week, drinking himself into oblivion. "What has your father done now?"

The smile upon Sebastian's face died. "He is who he is," he answered with a shrug. "Nothing he does surprises me, and yet...."

Leopold placed a comforting hand on his friend's shoulder. "And yet it never ceases to hit its mark," he finished for him. "Is Victoria all right?"

At the mention of his beloved little sister, Sebastian's jaw clenched. "She lives in a tomb," he snarled. "How can she ever be all right? Mother is barely a shadow of herself these days." He closed his eyes and inhaled a deep breath. "I swear," he gritted out through clenched teeth, "if he ever does dare do to Victoria what he did to my mother, I will..."

Leopold nodded, understanding only too well. The Earl of Weston, Sebastian's father, was a most unpleasant man. He cared neither for his wife nor for his children, only ever focused on his own desires and needs. "Very well," Leopold gave in, seeing the dark cloud hovering above his friend's head. "I suppose one drink will do no harm."

Slapping him on the shoulder, Sebastian laughed, "You have no idea, my friend! For I am a wolf in sheep's clothing, and if you are not careful, I will lead you down into hell."

Following his friend outside, Leopold wondered at the differences in their lives. In an odd way, Sebastian's bad fortune made Leopold feel even worse. Considering everything he had, he should be happy, should he not? And in a way, he was. However, something was missing, wasn't it? If only he knew what that was!

Ignoring the guilt slowly seeping into his heart, Leopold climbed into his friend's carriage and seated himself opposite him. Never in his life had he taken to drinking; however, today he saw no reason not to. After all, what harm could it do?

Chapter Two

WHISPERS OF KINSHIP

" I commend you on your lightness of foot, Miss Hayes," Lord Hefferton told her kindly, as he guided her across the dance floor. "I have yet to meet another who moves with more grace and comportment than you."

Maryann smiled at him demurely. "You are too kind, my lord."

The ballroom was crowded, and many guests had joined them on the dance floor. The air was a little stuffy, and Maryann was glad when someone pulled open the terrace doors to allow some cooling night air inside. Joyful voices echoed around them, and out of the corner of her eye, Maryann spotted her parents, standing off to the side, watching her most intently.

Indeed, they were still suspicious of her motives in encouraging Lord Hefferton's suit. Of course, Maryann had to admit that they were right.

The man was an earl and possessed a large fortune. As far as Maryann was aware, only a small portion of it was needed to cover her family's debts. Still, despite his position, Lord Hefferton had proved to be a kind and respectful man. He was always calm and collected, always observed proper manners and never ever stepped out of line.

Even if she could never love him, Maryann felt certain that he would make her a good husband. He would never raise his voice nor his hand against her. He would treat her with respect and allow her to run their home independently...so long as she adhered to proper rules.

From what Maryann had observed, Lord Hefferton did not seek a bride in possession of a large dowry or title–for he himself possessed both–but instead valued proper decorum and behaviour that was beyond reproach. He himself possessed a sparkling white reputation, and he intended for his wife to uphold it all the same.

When the dance ended, Lord Hefferton escorted her back to her parents. He offered her a respectful bow, and then turned to her father. "Lord Everleigh," he addressed her father with the utmost dignity, "would you allow me to call upon your daughter on the morrow?"

With a bit of a tense look upon his face, Maryann's father gave his permission, then turned to her the moment Lord Hefferton took his leave. "Does he truly suit you, my dear?" Doubt rested in his eyes.

Maryann willed a smile onto her face. After having done so repeatedly over the past few months, she felt quite confident that it was convincing. "Of course, he does," she told her father. "He is a most kind and deserving man, and I enjoy our dances most...ardently."

Her parents simply looked at her, not bothering to comment upon their daughter's statement. Then her mother cast her a warm smile, looped her arm through her husband's and said to her, "Enjoy yourself, my dear. We shall be right over there." Then she led her husband away. "Come. I saw a dear acquaintance arriving just now." And off they walked, leaving Maryann to look after them.

Exhausted, Maryann felt her shoulders slump briefly before she reminded herself to uphold pretences at all times. Lord Hefferton would not appreciate it if he saw her slouching in a corner. What kind of image would that represent?

Turning abruptly, Maryann collided with a young woman, whose dainty foot unfortunately ended up under Maryann's slipper.

An exclamation of pain escaped the golden-haired lady, her eyes going wide as she shrank back.

"Oh, dear!" Maryann exclaimed, clasping her hands over her mouth. "I'm so terribly sorry. Have I injured you gravely?"

Moving her foot, stretching and bending it, the young woman waved Maryann's concerns away. "Oh, it was nothing, I assure you."

Maryann breathed a sigh of relief. "Are you certain? Perhaps you should sit. Can I fetch you a drink?"

The young woman laughed, "I am perfectly fine. There is no need for you to worry." She set down her foot, testing it repeatedly, almost bouncing in her step proving that she was indeed fine. "See?"

"I hope you will still be able to dance," Maryann said, concerned that she had ruined the young woman's evening.

"Oh, these days I do not dance much," her unexpected companion replied, a hint of regret in her voice though. Her blue eyes drifted across the room to linger momentarily on a tall, raven-haired, rather tense-looking gentleman. "This past year I've rarely had occasion to dance." She blinked, and her gaze moved back to Maryann, a small smile beginning to play upon her lips. "Being a new mother makes everything else seem far less important."

Maryann returned the young woman's smile. "Congratulations...," she paused as she realized that she did not know the woman's name.

"Call me Leonora," the golden-haired woman offered with a deep smile. "Life is far too short to stand on ceremony, I find."

Maryann laughed, enjoying the sound as well as the feeling, realizing in that moment that simple joy had been all but absent from her life these past few months. "I'm Maryann."

Together, the two women ventured to the refreshment table and procured themselves a chilled glass of lemonade. Then they continued on, moving through the crowded room until they stepped out onto the terrace, welcoming the cooling night air.

"The gentleman you were dancing with," Leonora inquired with a sidelong glance at Maryann, "does he hold meaning to you?"

Maryann inhaled a deep breath, not certain how to reply.

Leonora nodded. "Ah, I see."

Turning to look at the woman beside her, Maryann paused, tempted to confide in another, but equally worried that the woman she had stumbled upon might somehow be connected to Lord Hefferton. "Are you acquainted with him?"

Leonora shook her head, her kind blue eyes turning toward

Maryann. "You need not worry," she assured her. "I shall not breathe a word of what you tell me to anyone. All I meant was that I'm familiar with your situation. I know what it is to choose a husband for a reason other than love." A hint of sadness lingered in her eyes, and she breathed in a wistful breath.

Maryann stilled, looking at the woman before her before turning to glance over her shoulder, her gaze falling once more on the dark-haired man she had seen before. "Your husband...?" Maryann paused, uncertain what to ask.

Leonora briefly bowed her head before she straightened, the markings of an iron will showing on her features. "He is a wonderful man," she whispered into the night air. "He dotes upon...our daughter. He is everything I always dreamed of in a husband." Her blue eyes swung around to meet Maryann, and what was written there told quite a different story than her words had.

Maryann smiled, feeling the sudden need to cheer up this woman, who had been so kind to her. "Being a mother, is it a blessing as they say?"

Instantly, the woman's face transformed, utter joy coming to her eyes. "She is my world," whispered Leonora, her face glowing. "She is worth every regret, every wrong decision, every wrong path taken." For a moment, she lifted her face to the night sky and closed her eyes. "It feels good to say it out loud," she whispered then. "I thank you for your company tonight." Turning to look at Maryann, Leonora reached out and gently placed her hand upon Maryann's arm. "Should you ever wish to speak...about anything, I would feel most honoured if you called on me." She glanced over Maryann's shoulder, and her hand tensed. "My husband is the Duke of Kensington." Her gaze returned to Maryann, and a small smile flitted across her face. "Just in case."

Overwhelmed by this offer, Maryann wondered if it would be wise to entertain thoughts of befriending this young woman, of confiding in her. For whether or not she wished to walk down this path, there was no other choice, was there? Her only option was to marry Lord Hefferton.

What good would it do to speak about her heart's desire? Not even in the quiet privacy of her own chamber did Maryann dare whisper of it to herself. After all, it would only point out that her heart and mind were guiding her down different paths, and she could not risk being swayed from the one she had chosen.

"I thank you for your kind offer," Maryann told the young woman, who looked at her with an expression that whispered of kinship. "You are most generous."

A part of Maryann wished she could go, wished she could take Leonora up on her offer. Always had she longed for a dear friend to confide in, but life had never brought her such. As an only child, she had only ever had her parents, unable to connect to other young ladies on a deeper level. Could Leonora be a friend? If Maryann could not have a husband she loved, then perhaps a friend would be the one comfort she could allow herself.

It was something to consider.

Chapter Three

A LADY IN SHINING ARMOUR

Maryann's heart pounded against her ribs as she quietly sneaked down the stairs. She cast a careful glance over her shoulder, but could only see dim outlines of the front hall as it lay quiet in the dark of night.

"Oh, this is a bad idea," she mumbled to herself, her eyes darting left and right for she expected someone, anyone, to come upon her at any moment. "This is a very bad idea."

And yet, Maryann did not stop. Why, she did not know. Still, an invisible force propelled her onward, across the foyer and out the front door. For a moment, a very distracted part of her mind wondered if she perhaps ought to have taken the servants' entrance; however, she found herself out on the pavement only moments later.

Fortune seemed to smile upon her for as she craned her neck, looking up and down the quiet street, she found it utterly deserted. Not a soul walked nearby. Not a single carriage rolled down the street. All she could hear was a soft trilling of some night bird as well as the wind rustling through the trees.

As the clouds moved, moonlight filtered through the canopy overhead, illuminating the street. The sudden brightness felt like a slap to Maryann, and she quickly pulled her hood farther down into her face.

A hint of panic raced down her spine, and for the thousandth time, she asked herself, "Are you mad? Have you lost all reason? What are you doing out here?"

Maryann could not say that she had an answer to these questions, least of all a good one. Still, her feet continued to carry her down the pavement, increasing the distance between herself and the only home she had ever known step-by-step.

In her mind's eye, Maryann continued to see the corner where her late grandfather had caught her in his arms one day when she had been only a child, twirling her around, laughing. It had been a moment of utter peace, of innocence and beauty. Maryann remembered it vividly as though it had happened the day before. In that moment, she had felt as though the world was hers, as though nothing was impossible. It had been an insignificant moment by outward standards. To her, however, it was one of the dearest memories she possessed.

The wind stirred, tugging on her cloak, and Maryann wrapped it more tightly around herself. She could hear the soft sound of her shoes upon the pavement, wondering if anyone else could hear it, if anyone else was nearby. "This is madness," she mumbled yet again, but kept walking.

Always had Maryann enjoyed looking at the stars with her grandfather. They had seemed vast and eternal and beautiful...because he had been there. The world had always seemed grander, safer and more beautiful with him by her side.

Glancing upward, she swept her gaze over the midnight canvas, a small smile tugging on her lips as she beheld the twinkling lights above. She could almost hear her grandfather's voice next to her. She could almost feel his presence.

Almost.

Earlier tonight, Maryann had contemplated simply heading out into the garden. Often had they spent time out there, watching the stars. Her mother had always called them night owls, a slight chuckle drifting from her lips. Still, tonight, Maryann knew that simply venturing outside into the garden would not be enough.

But perhaps if she stood in that place...at that corner...and looked up at the stars.

Maryann heaved a deep sigh. Her heart was in an uproar. Her mind was utterly confused. Her body seemed unable to stop trembling. She knew what she had to do, and yet, it seemed that a part of her would not allow her to go through with her plan. She needed reassurance. She needed courage. She needed her grandfather.

Always had he managed to calm each and every fear that had ever assailed her. Perhaps, tonight, if she stood in that one place, at that one corner, where all of her memories of him seemed bundled, perhaps then her pulse would finally calm and allow her to breathe again.

After all, her family's well-being depended upon it. She needed to be calm and collected; but right now, right here, she was anything but.

The sound of a carriage rumbling down the street, which crossed to the one she was on farther up ahead, sent a chill all the way down to her bones. Maryann flinched and shrank back into the shadows, her heart pounding even more wildly than it had before. What if she stumbled upon someone? What if a thief lay in wait in the shadows? What if she never made it back home?

Her fingernails dug into the palms of her hands and she forced herself to abandon these dark thoughts. Her feet continued onward as Maryann willed her mind to think of nothing else but the promise of solace. Oh, how much she needed it! Never before had she needed it as much as she did in this very moment.

She would simply have to hope that she would not cross another's path this night.

The drunken laughter of his peers echoed to Leopold's ears. He and Sebastian sat in a darkened corner of the club, a good distance from a group of gentlemen loudly discussing the newest bets as well as their possible outcomes. Smoke and the scent of spirits lingered in the air, and no matter how often Leopold turned his head to let his gaze sweep over men he had known his entire life, he always felt disappointment instead of companionship.

"I cannot rightly say that you look any better than before," commented Sebastian with a slurred snicker. "Not that I had expected you to, mind you. But hope is generally the last thing to go."

Leopold pushed his glass farther up onto the table, realizing something he had in truth already known the moment he had sat down at this very table hours ago; that sulking in his misery would not see the mantle of it draped upon his shoulders slide to the floor. "Why do you come here?" he asked his friend, unable to imagine spending his life in this manner.

Sebastian shrugged. "That I cannot say." He heaved a long sigh, and despite the fogginess in his mind, Leopold could see that his friend tried his best to appear positive. "Perhaps it is simply that I cannot think of another place to go. At least here, I sometimes am able to forget."

Leopold frowned, rubbing his hands over his eyes. He blinked and tried to see through the blurriness, his gaze fixed upon his friend, who slowly came into focus. "Can you not simply take your mother and sister out into the country?"

Slumping forward, Sebastian snorted, "He would never allow it."

"Why?"

"How am I to know?" Sebastian shook his head, his hands lifted in bafflement as he stared across the table at Leopold. "The man likes misery, and he particularly likes it when he has others to force it upon." A painful darkness rang in his voice, and Leopold understood that it was the hopelessness of his situation that weighed so heavily upon Sebastian's shoulders.

"Has he threatened to disown you?"

Sebastian shrugged his shoulders. "The man has threatened a number of things on a number of occasions. You cannot truly expect me to recall them all." Sighing, he downed the contents of his glass in one swallow. "I am nothing without him," he whispered, looking up and meeting Leopold's eyes. "Of that, he reminds me daily. Even if I wished, which of course I do, to take my sister and also my mother away from him, I have nothing. He owns me. I am his heir, his chess piece." He buried his face in his hands.

A heavy weight settled upon Leopold's heart, seeing his friend in such misery, misery that burned like a raging fire compared to the little candle he called his own. "Why do you not simply leave?"

Sebastian's eyes were bloodshot as he looked up. "I could never leave her," he whispered solemnly, determination steeling his eyes. "She is mine to protect, and I will do so as best as I can."

Leopold nodded, knowing very well how deeply Sebastian cared for his little sister.

For a good long while, the two men simply sat there, not speaking, simply waiting for time to tick by. Then Leopold pushed to his feet, suddenly unable to bear this depressive sense of desperation a moment longer. "Will you come with me?"

Sebastian blinked, then looked at him. "And go where?"

Leopold nodded. "Good night then, old friend. I hope I shall see you in better spirits tomorrow." He stepped away from the table, his feet rather unsteady.

"I wouldn't count on it," Sebastian chuckled darkly.

Stepping outside into the cold night air, Leopold inhaled a deep breath. The chill chased itself down into his lungs, an invigorating feeling if ever he had known one. Again, he rubbed his hands over his face, trying to clear his mind and chase away the fog that still lingered. He glanced up and down the darkened street, his eyes squinting at the light from the streetlamps. Then he set one foot in front of the other, slowly making his way down the pavement. His head seemed to be spinning. On top of it, it felt heavier than he remembered. His feet too were as lead, and he felt as though he were trudging through water as he made his way down the street.

All the while, that forlorn look upon his friend's face stayed with him. Sebastian truly had a life most trying, and Leopold wondered how *he* would have dealt with it if he had found himself in such a situation. As it was, Leopold could not even handle the happy life he had been granted. Was he even fit to be the next marquess?

It was that thought, the thought to fail others, others who depended upon him, upon his judgment, his wisdom, his knowledge of the world, that terrified him the most. His father was an awe-inspiring man in every way. What if Leopold could never fill his shoes?

Leopold kept his eyes fixed on the next corner, knowing he would need to round it. It seemed such a simple feat, something he did every day without thought, something a child could do, something no one would consider an accomplishment. Still, as his feet moved him forward, Leopold worried that they might not be able to perform the task.

Leaning slightly left, Leopold tried to encourage his feet to change direction. For a short moment, it seemed as though it might work. His body turned, his feet carrying him where he wanted to go. And then a dark shadow suddenly appeared out of nowhere, brushing against his shoulder and offsetting his balance completely.

As though his feet had been knocked out from under him, Leopold crashed to the ground, his right side connecting rather painfully with the unyielding pavement. A cry of pain tore from his lips, closely followed by a muttered curse.

"Oh, dear! I'm so sorry. Are you hurt?"

The voice came out of nowhere, sweet and melodious. It seemed to hover in the air, somewhere nearby, and Leopold stilled.

Still lying on his back, he blinked. Then his gaze moved, searching the darkness surrounding him. A shadow moved toward him, then knelt down by his side. He glimpsed a hooded figure, her face hidden in darkness. Her hands, however, moved to touch his face, then ran over his shoulders and arms. "Are you injured?"

Leopold tensed at her touch for it was startlingly sweet and sooth-ing, like a cooling breeze on a hot summer's day. "I'm fine," he croaked, wondering if it was the truth.

"That is a relief," the young woman exclaimed, her emotions only to evident in the soft swing of her voice. "Please, let me help you up."

Out of the dark, Leopold saw a slender hand reach out toward him. It was like a beacon, something that called to him, and Leopold reached for it without thought. Her skin felt cool against his own, smooth and soft; and unexpectedly, a part of him wished he would never have to let her go.

Her hand upon his tightened and she rose to her feet, leaning back and bracing herself to pull him to his own.

The world began to spin again as Leopold tried to stand. He fought a wave of dizziness and stumbled onward a few steps with great difficulty. Still, in that moment, failure was not an option. He had to stand. It was something incredibly simple. But here, in this moment, in front of her, with her hand in his, Leopold knew he could not fail.

He simply could not.

On trembling legs, Leopold stood, concentrating hard on maintaining his balance. It took him a moment to realize that his hands were clasped about her upper arms, keeping him from falling back to the ground. He stilled then and stared at her face, still shrouded in darkness from the hood that fell well into her face. "I'm sorry," he stammered, only now noticing the tension that held her body rigid. Of course, she had to be frightened, to be grasped by a stranger in the dark of night.

"Release me," she demanded then, her voice trembling slightly. Just as Leopold had known he could not fail to stand, he now knew that he could not release her. Something deep inside him urged him to hold on. "I'm afraid if I do so," he said, "I shall fall flat on my face."

"Are you injured after all?" she asked into the night's stillness. "Do you need help?"

"I'm not injured," he admitted honestly, "however, I have spent this night in a rather foolish way." He pinched his eyes shut against a wave of dizziness. "My head is spinning, and my knees have all but turned to water."

"You are inebriated," she observed, a hint of accusation in her voice.

"I'm afraid I am."

Inhaling a slow breath, she straightened her shoulders and lifted her head. Her hood slid back a little, revealing two full lips pressed into a tight line. "Release me!"

Sensing her fear, Leopold did as she had ordered. Slowly, he peeled back his fingers from their tight grip upon her arms. The instant his hold on her disappeared, he began to sway on his feet. The dizziness grew in intensity, and he felt certain that any moment now he would once again collide hard with the pavement under his feet.

However, no pain came, for instead of the hard ground, he felt soft hands grasp his arms. "You are in no condition to walk on your own," she observed with a tinge of regret as well as the aforementioned accusation in her voice. "Where do you live?"

Holding on to the young woman, Leopold nodded his head down the street, the movement sending a sharp pain through his left temple.

"Very well then," she said, turning in the direction he had indicated. "I shall see you home."

Leopold smiled at her in the dark. "You are my lady in shining armour," he chuckled, gazing down at her.

Her head rose then, and for the first time, Leopold found himself looking into two bright, blue eyes. A faint smile curled up her lips, and he heard a slight chuckle rumble in her throat. "That would make you my knight in distress," she pointed out with slightly raised brows.

Leopold laughed, trying his best to ignore the dull throb pounding against the inside of his skull. "As long as you save me, I do not object."

Her smile was radiant although hesitant. "You ought not have imbibed this much," she chided then, once more lowering her head as they proceeded onward another step or two.

"I agree."

Her head rose, and she looked up at him once more. "Then why did you?"

A long sigh slipped from Leopold's lips. He had not been able to explain himself sober; now, drunk beyond reason, what chance did he stand? "To forget," he mumbled, uttering the first words that came to mind.

"To forget what?" she prompted, a quizzical look upon her brows as she regarded him with unexpected interest.

Leopold shrugged. "Everything. Life. Duty and responsibility. Everything that is uncertain." He inhaled a deep breath as a wave of anger washed over him. "I wish I knew my path," he muttered in a moment of impatience and exasperation. "I wish life could be simple. I wish I knew how to live it...for myself as well as for others. I wish I didn't have to choose. I wish I knew what was right." He closed his eyes, a dark chuckle rumbling in his throat. "Self-pity certainly is an endearing quality, is it not?"

To his utter surprise, her face did not whisper of annoyance when he gazed upon it again. What he saw there was understanding.

Shockingly so.

Her chest rose and fell with a slow breath as her blue eyes gazed up into his. They lingered there for a long moment, searching, contemplating. Then she swallowed and her lips parted. "Uncertainty can be crippling indeed," she whispered as though not daring to speak any louder. Another slow breath moved her shoulders up and down as she gathered her thoughts. "To find oneself at a fork in the road..." Sighing, she shook her head.

Fascinated, Leopold watched her face, trying to understand the thoughts that lingered in her mind, the emotions that bloomed in her heart. There was something familiar about those bright blue eyes, looking past him into the dark night, thoughts reflected in them, which he knew only too well. "You too find yourself at a fork in the road, do you not?"

Her gaze returned from far away and resettled upon his. "Do we not all find ourselves in such a place now and then?"

Leopold nodded. "That is true. However, it is not always considered a heavy burden." His gaze swept her face. "What was it that chased you out into the night all by yourself?"

As though he had struck her, her eyes widened and snapped up to his face, staring at him in utter shock, a hint of concern swirling in her blue depths.

Leopold could only hope that she would not run from him now; still, he had to know.

He had to know *her*.

Chapter Four

A KNIGHT IN DISTRESS

Maryann stared up at the tall stranger. His large hands remained locked around her arms, keeping him upright as he half-leaned upon her. His nearness as well as the dark shrouding them in its black cloak sent a shiver crawling over her skin. Something deeply unsettling bloomed in her heart, uttering a warning, reminding her that the person she was with was not a friend, was not family, but a stranger. Someone she did not know. Someone who might well do her harm.

After all, London after dark was no place for a young woman on her own.

And yet, something else stirred in her heart as well.

As Maryann gazed up into the stranger's eyes, open and honest and whispering of the same need to have someone understand, she felt a deep longing to confide in another, to confide in him and be understood. Why, she could not say, but a part of her yearned to trust him, to answer his question and see what he would do with it.

Maryann inhaled a deep breath, praying that her instincts did not lead her astray. "My grandfather," she whispered, holding the stranger's yearning gaze.

Blinking rapidly, he swayed slowly from side to side before his eyes opened once more, again steady upon her own. "Grandfather?" he asked, confusion swirling in his eyes. Then his gaze moved from hers and he glanced around, suddenly flinching as no doubt a piercing pain jolted through his head. "Is he here with you?" he gritted out through clenched teeth, his eyes pinched shut once again.

Maryann waited for his pain to pass and his gaze to become steady once more. "He is not," she told him softly. "He died two years ago." Still, the memory of her grandfather remained at the forefront of her mind and always brought with it a wistful smile and a teary eye.

"I'm afraid I do not understand," said the stranger, the hint of an apologetic smile curling up the corners of his mouth. "Perhaps it is my head," he chuckled, then flinched once more. "Indeed, it seems frighteningly inadequate at present."

Maryann smiled at him, unable not to. Something about his honesty, his self-criticism was utterly endearing to her for she understood it well. "Before he died," she told him with a sigh, "he used to take me out into the night, and together we would watch the stars. We would talk about everything and nothing." Another wistful sigh left her lips, and she lifted a finger, wiping a tear from the corner of her eye. "Never in my life, have I felt as much at peace as I did in these moments, never as clear or level-headed, never as certain or even as dauntless." A slight chuckle escaped her lips as she remembered the daring twinkle in her grandfather's eye whenever she would dare voice doubt or uncertainty. *Life is not Maths*, he had always told her. *You cannot know what the result will be until you have lived each and every moment. So why worry? It will only make your head hurt.*

The stranger chuckled as though he, too, had been drawn back to relive her most precious memory. "You miss him," he whispered, and she felt his thumbs brush over her arms, back and forth, a soothing gesture.

It felt most intimate, and yet, Maryann was not afraid or worried. He might be a stranger, but he was also a decent man. She was certain of it.

"Did you watch the stars then?" the stranger asked gently. "Did your grandfather's memory help you?"

Closing her eyes, Maryann slowly shook her head. "I had hoped it would," she admitted. "Still, it is not the same without him. I could almost hear his voice, and yet, he was not there." She sighed, "I still don't know what to do."

For a long moment, his warm gaze lingered upon hers, his hands still holding onto her, the pads of his thumbs still brushing gently over her arms. Then he spoke, and it was no more than a whisper. "Is there anything I can do? Any help I can give you?" One corner of his mouth teased upward into a bit of a lopsided smile. "I'm aware I've not made the best impression tonight, however, if there's anything you need...?"

Maryann could see his deep desire to help her, to be of service, to make a difference. She could see that he, too, felt powerless in his life, like a piece of driftwood tossed about on the open ocean. "It is kind of you to offer," she told him gently, not wishing to disappoint him. "However, I know what I must do. I did even before I left the house tonight. I suppose all I wanted, all I was hoping for was peace of mind, the sense that I was doing the right thing." She smiled up at him, to assure him that she was well, wishing she could believe it, too.

"Did you find it?" Something more than curiosity showed in his eyes as he asked. Maryann had the distinct feeling that her answer was of the utmost importance to him as well. Perhaps he hoped that if she had found some kind of assurance, something that had told her which path to choose, it might work for him as well.

Offering him a sad smile, Maryann shook her head. "I'm afraid not. I'm still at odds about what to do. I have doubts. A part of me wishes that things could be different, and yet, I know that will never be the case. Life is what it is, and we simply have to accept it."

The stranger huffed out an exhausted breath. "That is indeed a frightening way to look at it," he pointed out, one eyebrow raised as he looked at her. "To be frank, I had hoped that there could be a way, that I would only have to look close enough, hard enough to find a way through this maze." He stilled, and his gaze swept her face once more. "May I ask...?" He hesitated; the look in his eyes, however, spoke volumes.

"You wish to know what my problem is, do you not?"

The stranger nodded, and once again flinched, squinting his eyes against the pain in his head.

"Marriage, of course," Maryann scoffed, unaware until this moment how infuriated she truly was with the situation she found herself in. "What other choice do women have these days?"

Inhaling a slow breath, the stranger watched her, his dark gaze tracing her drawn brows, lingering upon the tight line of her lips before once again moving upward and settling on her eyes. "You do not wish to marry?"

Maryann scoffed, "I wish for the choice to be mine."

"I see." The stranger's jaw hardened as though he were clenching his teeth. "Are you...under some pressure to make a choice you would rather not?"

Maryann felt her lips part. She was about to respond truthfully, honestly, without holding anything back. And to a stranger no less. Only in the last second was she able to force the words back down, to not say all that was on her mind, all that wanted to escape into the world. "I must head home soon," she mumbled, suddenly unable to meet his eyes as though her failure to respond somehow failed him.

His right hand moved upward on her arm until it brushed over her shoulder and then moved farther upward still, the tips of his fingers whispering by the delicate skin upon her neck. Maryann held her breath, and when his fingers grasped her chin, she lifted her eyes, unable not to. What an odd night this was!

For a seemingly endless moment, they stood out in the night, shrouded in darkness, strangers to one another. And yet, a part of Maryann knew that the stranger had seen inside her as she had not allowed anyone else before. She could not say why, but somehow, some part of her had come to trust him. How it had happened, she did not know, either. But it had.

Somehow, it had.

"I wish I could help you," the stranger whispered, his gaze still locked upon hers as though he wished to never let her go. It was a most unexpected feeling, but also strangely welcome. "Tell me what I can do. Please, I cannot bear the thought of us parting ways like this, of knowing that after tomorrow you will be forced down a path not of your choosing." His thumb gently brushed over her chin, a caress Maryann felt to the tips of her toes.

Tears collected in Maryann's eyes, and she furiously blinked them away, knowing that whatever she felt in this precious, rare, completely unexpected moment had no bearing on the days to come. "You are too kind," she whispered. "I do wish…" The words were left hanging in the still night air for Maryann did not know how to speak of what she wished. It was too much, too impossible. Something that only ever lived in dreams. Dreams she had not even known she possessed.

Not until today.

"I must go." Indeed, if she were found out here by herself in the company of a stranger, all her efforts would have been in vain. No doubt, Lord Hefferton would turn from her, disappointed by her lack of judgment, by her inappropriate behaviour, by all she was. "Do you think you will find your way on your own?"

The stranger sighed, and for a moment, his hand upon her arm seemed to tighten, speaking of the same reluctance she, too, felt. "It seems my head has cleared at least a little," he told her through clenched teeth. "I shall be fine. And you?" Slowly, tentatively, he lifted his head, no doubt in order to avoid more pain, and glanced around the darkened streets. "Do you live near here?"

Maryann nodded, using her free hand to dab at her eye. A most insistent tear had been lingering, and it would be of no use for her to shed it. "It is not far. I shall be there in a matter of moments." Then she reached up, and her hand settled upon his, gently urging him to release her.

For a moment, his hand tensed upon her chin. He seemed to be moving toward her or perhaps he was simply swaying on his feet still trying to keep his balance. Whatever it was, for a short, heart-rendering moment, Maryann thought that he would kiss her. And when he did not, when he finally released her and took an unsteady step back, her heart ached with regret.

Retreating a step of her own, Maryann busied herself by running her hands over the folds of her gown. She knew she ought to whisper a goodbye, turn around and head in the direction of the safety of her home. Still, she lingered, slowly lifting her gaze to meet the stranger's. "Will you be all right?" Indeed, she had already asked him that, had she not? Why was she lingering? Prolonging the moment?

A soft smile curled up the stranger's lips. "You have saved me indeed, oh, brave lady." He lifted a hand, unsteady and trembling, to run it through his hair, his dark gaze lingering on hers just the same. "If only there were a way for you to save yourself as well."

Maryann sighed, "Not until this moment have I allowed myself to wish for such an outcome." Looking at him, she shook her head in disapproval. "Speaking to you tonight made me realize what it is I genuinely want, wish for, hope for. How dare you," she chuckled despite the darkness slowly settling in her heart, "take away the hard-won determination I had even minutes ago to do what was right, to follow this path wherever it might lead me. If not happy, I was at least content; now I am not."

For a long moment, the stranger remained quiet. Then he took a careful step toward her. "Perhaps you were never content. Perhaps all I did was open your eyes to something you already knew."

Maryann nodded. "That may be true," she admitted reluctantly. "Still, it makes me think that sometimes ignorance is indeed bliss. It would have been simpler had I never realized the truth, then perhaps my life, my choice – what little I have of it – would have been easier to bear."

The stranger's jaw hardened as his gaze held hers. "Then make a different choice," he urged, insistence in his voice as though her choice affected him as much as her. "Whatever help I can give you, I shall. You have my word on that."

Wishing she could accept his offer, Maryann frowned up at him. "Why?" she asked, still bewildered by their encounter. "Why would you offer such a thing to me? I am no one to you. I am a stranger. Why would you do this?"

The stranger inhaled a slow breath, his gaze clearer than it had been all night. "By anyone else's standards, yes, you *should* be a stranger to me." For a second, his gaze became distant as though a memory had suddenly found its way to the forefront of his mind. "Only the day before, my father told me that life should not be about what we *should* do, but about what we want to do." He sighed, "I admit I don't quite understand the full meaning of his words yet, but I know beyond the shadow of a doubt what advice he would give you. The same he gave me." He stilled, and once again his gaze moved to some faraway place only he could see. "His words make more sense to me now. Somehow, I could not understand them before, but now..." He smiled at her, and the warmth of his smile felt like a balm to her chilled skin. "You saved me in more ways than one. I thank you, oh, brave lady."

Maryann chuckled, loving the way he teased her. "Should you ever need saving again, call on me," she whispered without thought, realizing too late that after tonight their paths must never cross again. For if they did, it would surely ruin her life, ruin everything she had worked for, everything she still thought necessary, everything she now knew she did not want. "I truly must go now." She took another step back and another; still, it felt as though she were fighting against the pull of a magnet, keeping her from breaking free.

Or perhaps she simply didn't want to.

"Good night," the stranger whispered, lifting a hand in a gesture of farewell. Even in the dark of night, with only the light of the streetlamps and the sliver of moon up in the sky, she could see the reluctance to bid her farewell on his face. He, too, wished that their paths would lead them in the same direction, but he, too, knew that it was impossible.

Before she could change her mind, Maryann tore her eyes away and then spun on her heel, rushing down the street that would lead her home. Tears stung her eyes anew. Where they came from, she did not know. Neither did she know what they meant; however, her heart ached most ardently. The thought that she would never again lay eyes on the stranger was utterly heart-breaking. How was this possible? An hour ago, she had not even known he existed, and now?

Her grandfather's voice suddenly echoed in her mind. *Some moments are fleeting and pass without a thought while others change the course of the world and turn it upside down.*

Not until this very moment had Maryann known what he had tried to tell her, what he had meant. Her mind had grasped the foundation of the idea, but her heart had never truly felt its truth. But now, she knew. To her heart-breaking regret, now she understood.

Maryann wished she did not for it would make marrying Lord Hefferton all the more difficult. Now, she had doubts. Now, she had caught a glimpse of an alternative future. Now, there was a longing in her heart.

A longing she would have to silence for it would not serve her.

As Maryann slipped inside her father's townhouse, the one they would be forced to sell if she did not marry Lord Hefferton, tears continued to flow down her cheeks. No matter how often she wiped them away, they would simply keep coming, reminding her every step of the way of what she was giving up.

Throwing herself onto her bed, Maryann buried her face in her pillows, muffling the sobs that tore from her throat. "If only I had never met him. If only."

Chapter Five

A DREAM COME TRUE

His head hurt.

His head hurt as it never had before, at least not to his recollection.

Rolling over in his bed, Leopold groaned, pressing his palms to his eyes, hoping the pressure would alleviate the painful throbbing behind his temples. Unfortunately, the dull thud kept on coming, again and again, as though someone were knocking on the door to his mind. How on earth had he ended up in such a state?

Dimly, Leopold recalled Sebastian sitting across from him, a glass in his hand. It was not an unusual sight; however, the memory of such a sight was usually clear and focused, and not fuzzy and somehow blurred. It seemed like a dream, not like something that had truly happened.

With his hands still pressed to his face, Leopold allowed his thoughts to move onward, to stumble through the evening from fragment to fragment, piecing together the events of the previous night. He remembered that they had been at the club, speaking of dark memories, of fearful thoughts, of a worrisome future. He remembered the look of anguish in his friend's eyes as well as the sense of crippling uncertainty in his own heart. He remembered leaving the club, his feet barely carrying him in a straight line, his head spinning. He remembered stumbling onward nonetheless, and then he remembered...

Leopold stilled, his hands slowly slipping from his face as his eyes opened. He flinched as the bright light of a new day sent a searing pain through his head. Still, the dim recollection of a memory lingered.

One most unfamiliar.

Equally blurred and out of focus as the others.

A face in the dark.

Inhaling a slow breath, Leopold slowly turned onto his back, his eyes opening incrementally, then blinking rapidly, trying to make peace with the bright morning light. His mind, however, remained in the dark of night, his eyes sweeping over a face he had never seen before. A face most kind and understanding. A face that brought utter longing to his heart.

"Who was she?" Leopold whispered, his voice no more than a croak. He could not recall her name nor any other detail aside from her lovely face and the kind heart that beat in her chest. She had come to him in the dark, like an angel trying to save him. "My lady in shining armour." A slight frown descended upon Leopold's face. The phrase felt odd, and yet, it echoed with truth. Had he called her that?

For a long moment, Leopold lay perfectly still, staring up at the ceiling, his mind lingering on the fragmented memories of the previous night. Warmth filled his chest at the thought of her. Somehow, she had understood the confusion and concern that plagued him. In all likelihood, he had not explained himself well; still, she had been able to understand, an echo of his own thoughts only too visible in her wide blue eyes.

Closing his eyes, Leopold felt a smile tug on his lips as he allowed his mind to drift off, focused on the memory of her. Suddenly, he felt peaceful and calm and no longer in doubt. Questions still surged through his mind, but they no longer intimidated him, they no longer whispered of his imminent failure. Somehow, he now had faith in himself. How had this happened?

Leopold tensed when a new thought sneaked into his mind, one that brought fear and anger with it for it was a thought he could not bear. He well knew that he had been drunk out of his mind the night before; what if...what if *she* had merely been a figment of his imagination?

The mere thought of it made Leopold groan. It was like a physical pain in his chest, and every part of his body ached. The thought that she was not of this world was the bleakest one he had had in a long, long time. He could not imagine never looking into those eyes again, never having them look back into his knowing that he was not alone, that there was a kindred soul, someone who understood.

But was there?

From Sebastian, he knew that spirits often addled the mind. How often had his friend spoken to him of strange dreams and odd scenes that had never taken place except in his mind? Countless times was the answer.

Had last night been one of those times for Leopold? Did his lady in shining armour not even exist? Was there not even the slightest chance that he would stumble upon her once again: somewhere, someplace, some time? The thought made him want to spend the rest of his life in his bed, turned away from the world and everyone in it. It was a cowardly, weak thought, but Leopold could not help it. Last night, he had found unexpected strength in a moment when he had least expected it, and the morning light had ripped it away.

He was devastated.

The next few days where the hardest Leopold had ever experienced. He felt tired, exhausted. His limbs were heavy. He felt as though he was trotting through water, sluggish and weighted down. Sadness lingered, and yet, a spark of hope remained for Leopold simply could not bring himself to accept that she did not exist, that she never had. And so, wherever he went, he found himself looking for her, his gaze sweeping the crowd, traveling from face to face, hoping, praying, wishing.

And then one night, when he had all but given up hope, he stepped into Hefferton's ballroom, and the impossible happened.

There she was.

Those eyes, he would have recognized them anywhere. That smile, tentative, and yet, full of determination, called to him, and he was lost.

Lost in the sight of her.

Like a fool, he stood and stared across the ballroom, his gaze lingering in a way it should not, sweeping over her face, once again familiarizing himself with the many emotions that rested in those soulful eyes. "She's real," he whispered to himself, unable not to, somehow needing to hear the words spoken out loud, even if only in hushed tones. "She's here."

"Who are you staring at?"

Leopold flinched at the sound of his brother's voice so close behind him. He had all but forgotten the world around him and now reluctantly re-joined their ranks. "No one," Leopold lied as he took a step back and turned to his brother, willing his gaze not to move back to his lady in shining armour.

Frederick chuckled, disbelief in his eyes as well as amusement. "Is that so?" Unerringly, his gaze travelled across the ballroom to the woman Leopold was trying hard to ignore. An impossible feat! "Who is she?" his brother asked, not being fooled by Leopold's attempts to hide something he himself could not quite understand yet.

His jaw tensed as he tried to think of something to say. For a reason he could not name, a part of him did not wish to divulge the events of a couple of nights ago to anyone. Not even his brother.

An easy smile upon his face, Frederick clasped a companionable hand on Leopold's shoulder. "You are an awful liar," his brother chuckled, and his gaze once more darted across the ballroom. "She is radiant, and you are quite obviously falling for her." His dark gaze returned to Leopold's. "Why would you try and hide that? I'm your brother; I would never tease you, or would I?" Again, he chuckled.

Leopold heaved a deep sigh. "I don't even know her name," he admitted in a hushed tone, worried that someone else might overhear.

A deep frown came to Frederick's face. "I could've sworn..." His voice trailed off. "You have never exchanged a word with her?"

Of its own volition, the right corner of Leopold's mouth quirked upward.

Seeing it, a deep smile snuck onto Frederick's face. "Then you have?" He took a step closer, his eyes narrowing, trying to look deeper. "You've spoken with her...and yet...you do not know her name? I must admit, I am most intrigued, dear brother. Tell me, how is it that you two know each other without ever having exchanged names?"

Leopold's lips thinned, and he glared at his brother. "This is not a jest, Frederick. If you intend to poke fun—"

"You misunderstand me," his brother interrupted, all humour gone from his face, replaced by a seriousness Leopold had rarely seen in him. "I can see that you care for her." He spoke quietly, his gaze holding Leopold's. "I can tell from the way you look at her." Slowly he shook his head, each movement from side to side emphasizing his words. "I would never poke fun at you, not about something like this, not when she is so important to you. All I ask is that you share your life with me. I am your brother, and as immature as I might seem sometimes, I will always stand at your side. I hope you can believe that."

Touched by his brother's solemn words, Leopold held his gaze.

Indeed, the youth, who had always had a head full of mischief, his thoughts always on the next adventure, responsibility something unknown to him, seemed to have grown up. There was something deeply serious, something caring, even something selfless in the way Frederick was looking at him now. "Very well," Leopold began, holding his brother's gaze to make him understand how earnest the situation was. "But you must promise me that you will not breathe a word of what I am about to tell you to anyone. Is that understood?"

His brother nodded, not making a jest or grinning foolishly.

Pulling Frederick to the side, Leopold explained about the night he had gone out with Sebastian and then ended up drunk on London's streets in the dark, all but stumbling over his lady in shining armour. Recounting these events made them seem like a fairy-tale, and Leopold felt compelled to glance over across the ballroom again and again, his eyes seeking her as she stood with an elderly couple, now and then exchanging a word.

"She was all by herself?" Frederick demanded, his eyes wide, utter surprise only too visible in them. "Are you saying she sneaked out of the house?"

Leopold could not help but feel a bit ruffled by the hint of indignation in his brother's voice; however, what bothered him more, he realized, was that he did not know. Yes, it was most likely that she had sneaked out of the house. Still, he did not know. He had not asked the specifics, and she had not volunteered them. "She was out to look at the stars," he told his brother, remembering the wistful expression upon her face as she had spoken to him of her grandfather.

All of a sudden, his memories of that night were inexplicably vivid.

"And you believe her?" A bit of an apologetic look came to Frederick's eyes; still, what Leopold read on his face was mostly concern. Concern for him, his brother. Leopold could not fault him for that, but he could defend *her*.

"Beyond the shadow of a doubt," he replied without a moment's hesitation.

Frederick smiled. "You seem quite taken with her, big brother." He took a step back, darting a look across the dance floor once more. "What do you intend to do?" A challenging gleam rested in Frederick's eyes, and Leopold had no trouble understanding his brother's words for what they were.

Inhaling a deep breath, Leopold straightened. "I intend to speak to her." Never in his life had Leopold felt braver and more terrified at the same time. Still, what he also knew beyond the shadow of a doubt was that he could not allow her to slip through his fingers again. Now, that he knew she was real and not merely a figment of his imagination, Leopold knew that he had to know her.

He could not allow this day to end without knowing her name. Never had he felt more certain about anything before.

And so, he smiled at his brother, prayed he would be able to string more than two words together in her presence and then marched across the dance floor, his gaze fixed on his lady in shining armour.

Chapter Six

A RETURN TO REALITY

"Are you certain you're all right, my dear?" Maryann's mother inquired, her brows slightly drawn in concern as her gaze swept over her daughter's face. "You look rather pale, and you've hardly said a word since we arrived."

At his wife's words, her father took a step closer to her, his own gaze narrowing, watching her. "Your mother is right. Are you feeling ill? Do you wish to return home?"

Willing the smile upon her face not to falter, Maryann turned to her parents. "I am perfectly fine," she assured them, wondering if they too could hear the hint of shrillness in her voice. "I was merely wool-gathering. That is all." Still, her hands trembled slightly, and she wished for a moment alone, without her parents observing every twitch, every sigh, every shadow falling over her face. "I believe I just saw a young lady whose acquaintance I've made the other night. Why do you and Father not step outdoors for a moment for a spell of fresh air?"

At her suggestion, her mother's gaze narrowed even farther. Suspicion rested in her grey eyes; still, she nodded her head, slipped her hand through her husband's arm and then urged him out of doors.

Watching them leave, Maryann sighed. The breath rushed from her lungs and back in again as the strain to uphold this mask, to keep it fixed in place at all times, fell from her. The muscles in her face began to ache from the strain she had placed on them, and she felt the soft sting of tears collecting in the corners of her eyes.

Clenching her hands, Maryann blinked her eyes rapidly, trying to dispel not only her tears but also that feeling of inevitability that had not left her side ever since...

The moment her eyes opened, Maryann's heart stopped.

For right there, only halfway across the ballroom, was he. The stranger she had met in the night. The man she had felt a strange kinship to. The one person she felt understood her perfectly.

As though to prove that it was still there, her heart picked up its pace, suddenly beating too fast, and yet, appropriately for the mere sight of him upended her world. Her eyes were all but glued to his. She could not blink. She could not look away. Step-by-step, he moved closer, his gaze never veering from hers, unaware of the dancers around him. He only had eyes for her as she only had eyes for him. It felt like a curse, a sickness, something she wished she could shake, but knew she was helpless against. It was a powerful feeling; if only she could enjoy it, if only...

And then he was there, right in front of her, those warm, knowing eyes looking down into hers. The corners of his mouth twitched, whispering of unexpected joy, of something overwhelming, an echo of her own emotions. "I half expected you to have been a dream."

His words brought a deep smile to Maryann's face, and she spoke without thought. "A good one, I hope?"

A deep sigh left his lips, and he moved a little closer or perhaps he was merely swaying on his feet. "The very best," he whispered as though sharing a most intimate feeling. "One-of-a-kind. One unlike any I have ever had."

Holding his gaze, the intensity she saw there almost overwhelming, Maryann exhaled a shuddering breath.

For a long moment, silence lingered between them. Then another small smile quirked upon his lips. "We've met under the most extraordinary circumstances," he whispered, casting a careful glance at their surroundings, ensuring that no one was within earshot. "Only much too late did I realize that I had not even bothered to ask your name." His smile deepened as he looked at her.

The look upon his face was so endearing, so teasing, so honest, that Maryann could not help but laugh. "As did I," she admitted, feeling a new warmth rush to her cheeks. "A regret most deeply felt."

"And yet you fail to answer me," her stranger pointed out with a smirk.

Maryann grinned up at him. "And you have yet to ask, my knight in distress."

Her stranger laughed; it was a warm, deep sound, intoxicating and tantalizing. "You are quite right, my lady." He offered her a formal bow, joy and delight lighting up his eyes. "Would you kindly share the secret of your name with me?"

Maryann offered him a slight courtesy, feeling like a young girl again playing at knights and princesses. "As you have asked with such honest ardour, I shall not deny you." Another breath left her lips as she gathered her wits. "I am Maryann Hayes."

"It is a pleasure to meet you, Miss Hayes," he greeted her, and while his words were simple, his eyes spoke of a much deeper regard as they held hers.

Maryann waited a heartbeat, then two, then three, but he remained silent. "And you, sir knight? Pray tell, what is your name? "

He chuckled, "Ah, you *do* care," he teased as though they had known each other for many years.

Maryann wanted to slap him good-naturedly upon the arm, surprising herself by the mere notion of it. "Of course, I wish to know. How could you ever think I did not?"

His grin broadened, and again he moved closer ever so slightly. "Leopold Lancaster," he said in a soft voice, his gaze never veering from hers, "Earl of Bentham."

"Leopold," Maryann whispered without thought. Then, when realization dawned of what she had done, she clasped her hands over her mouth, her eyes widening in shock at the familiarity she had assumed. "I do apologize, my lord."

"There is nothing to apologize for," the young earl assured her, the warmth in his gaze proving his words true. "In fact, I admit I much prefer it. Will you call me Leopold?"

"I'm not certain it would be appropriate," Maryann objected, knowing she ought to, but wishing for the opposite.

"You may well be right," he agreed before a teasing twinkle lit up his eyes. "We must keep it a secret then, something shared only between the two of us."

Maryann felt a shiver dance down her back. "What you suggest, my Lord, is indeed most scandalous."

Leopold laughed. "I cannot say that I have much experience in this area," he chuckled. "All my life, I have tried to do what is right, to play by the rules, and do the best I could." He inhaled a slow breath. "Now, however, I find that I've grown tired of other people's rules. You helped me see it. Now, I wish to do what *I* deem right." Again, he chuckled, a tinge of uncertainty in his voice. "I'm certain it will take practice. It still feels strange, very strange, but I'm confident that I shall master it."

His words spoke to Maryann and echoed within her heart. Oh, how she wished she had the same freedom! What was it like to be able to choose freely? Was he free to choose a bride according to his own designs? Or was he, too, bound by certain expectations? Was that not the way of the world?

"What do you say?" Leopold whispered, and Maryann belatedly realized that at least in her thoughts she was already calling him by his first name.

Unable to hide the smile slowly spreading over her face, Maryann nodded. "I believe I shall not be able to prevent myself from addressing you thus. Your name seems to sit at the tip of my tongue, demanding to be uttered."

A look of deepest joy came to his face. "Will you grant me permission then to use your name as well...Maryann?"

"How can I refuse? It would only be fair, would it not?"

"And most pleasurable," Leopold pointed out with a smirk. "Would you like to dance?" He held out his hand to her, and never in her life had Maryann wanted anything more.

Still, she hesitated when thoughts of what you ought to do

returned. Her gaze broke from his and worriedly swept the crowd, searching for Lord Hefferton. Was he watching her right now? Had she already lost his regard by conversing with Leopold in a most intimate manner? Had she already ruined everything she had worked so hard for these past months?

"Is something wrong?" Leopold asked, his voice suddenly tense as he moved closer.

Maryann could feel his gaze sweeping her face, trying to look closer, trying to understand. Afraid to see disappointment in his eyes, Maryann swallowed hard before she finally lifted her gaze to meet his. "You might not recall," she began, remembering his state of inebriation the night they had met, "but I already told you that..." More words would not come. Instead, tears collected in her eyes.

Moments ticked by as they looked at one another.

Confusion rested in Leopold's eyes before a slight frown began to draw down his brows, becoming more pronounced second by second as understanding dawned. "I may not remember every detail of that night," he began tentatively, his jaw suddenly clenched as he forced out the words, "but I seem to remember you speaking of marriage and having the choice removed from your hands." His lips thinned, and he seemed to be putting up a great effort to remain still. "Are you betrothed?"

Maryann felt as though she were a messenger of doom. The words lodged in her throat, and yet, she knew she had to say them. She had to tell him the truth, lest he hoped for something that could never be. "As good as."

Those three little words drained the blood from his face as he stared down at her, shock freezing his features.

Maryann felt awful and delighted at the same time. It pained her to see him thus, but at the same time, it made her heart soar to know that he genuinely cared for her even after only such a short, very short acquaintance. It had been a powerful moment that night as this one now was as well, but not powerful enough to alter what was.

"Ah, Miss Hayes, there you are."

Maryann flinched at the sound of Lord Hefferton's voice. Her head snapped around, her eyes wide, and she all but stared at him for a second too long, wondering how much he had seen and heard.

Seeing her shock, his brows furrowed. "Are you well? You seem out of sorts? Is there anything you require?" His kindness made Maryann's heart ache even more, making guilt flood her being. Lord Hefferton deserved better. Better than her, but she could not simply give up what a union with him promised to her family. "I'm quite well, my lord," she assured him, forcing a small smile onto her face. She kept her gaze fixed on Lord Hefferton, unable to look at Leopold, afraid of what she would see.

Lord Hefferton nodded, then turned his gaze to her companion. "Bentham," he greeted Leopold, offering him a polite smile. "How good to see you here."

Beside her, Maryann felt Leopold shift from one foot onto another, his arms moving to link behind his back. "I thank you kindly for the invitation," he replied in a polite voice; however, Maryann could hear the tension that lingered. "It is a marvellous evening, and I was just saying to Miss Hayes," even with her head slightly bowed, Maryann could all but feel him look at her, "how truly magnificent your renovations have been. You truly have spared no expense."

Maryann barely heard the short exchange of the two men about the house and its gardens. Her heart was pounding, and the blood rushed in her ears. Never in her life had she felt torn in such a way.

"Do you feel well enough to dance?" Lord Hefferton asked, holding out his arm to her. "Or would you rather take a stroll through the gardens? Fresh air might do you good."

Wishing she could accept Leopold's arm instead, Maryann turned to Lord Hefferton. Although the idea of fresh air was a most welcome one, Maryann did not feel like conversing with him. A dance might prove more diverting. "I feel quite well," she lied, smiling up at him as best as she could. "A dance would be most welcome."

Lord Hefferton returned her smile. "As you wish." As she slipped her hand through the crook of his arm, he turned to look at Leopold and gave him a quick nod of the head. "Bentham."

Maryann could hear Leopold mumble "Hefferton" as her future betrothed led her away in the direction of the dance floor.

Maryann felt ill.

Chapter Seven

THE ONE QUESTION

L eopold stared after her, a sudden sense of possessiveness coming over him seeing Maryann on the arm of another man. She did not turn to meet his gaze, and from the way she kept her head bowed, he knew that Lord Hefferton was not Maryann's choice. Then why was she choosing him? Or had her parents chosen him for her?

Sighing, Leopold raked a hand through his hair, realizing that he knew next to nothing about her. Until a few minutes ago, he had not even known her name. There was no reason to feel for her as he felt. She was a stranger to him. They had met and spoken a grand total of two times. And yet, in her company, he felt at peace. He felt like himself, and the moment she walked away, it was as though she took that certainty with her.

"You look like a vengeful god, big brother," Frederick commented with a chuckle as he and his two friends walked up to him. "A vengeful god about to destroy the world in his anger."

Leopold exhaled an exasperated sigh, then glared at his brother. "I'd appreciate it if you laughed about someone else."

Instantly, Frederick's face sobered. "I am not laughing," he said solemnly. "Believe it or not, I'm trying to help you for I know that you are not one to make hasty decisions." He exchanged a look with his childhood friends Oliver Cornell, Earl of Cullingwood, and Kenneth Moreton, Viscount Hutchins, who both nodded in agreement. "If you want her, you need to move fast."

Leopold turned to stare at his brother, dumbstruck by what he had just heard. "What do you mean?"

Oliver chuckled, his eyes lighting up with the usual mirth. "It would seem, she has addled your mind in the most profound way. Women have a way of doing so without effort, I assure you." He laughed.

Leopold's jaw hardened. "She has done nothing of the kind!" he snapped at his brother's friend.

Frederick placed a hand on Leopold's shoulder, his gaze seeking his brother's. "Ignore him," he said with a sideways glance at Oliver. "All I meant to say was that it is clear that you care for her. It is also rather obvious that you have a competitor." His brows rose in challenge. "Now, what do you intend to do?"

Suddenly feeling defeated, Leopold threw up his arms. "There is nothing I can do. She told me she's as good as engaged."

"As good as," Oliver exclaimed as he pushed forward and came to stand next to Frederick, "is not engaged yet. There is still a chance...if you choose to take it."

Frederick nodded, exchanging a look with Kenneth, who had remained quiet thus far. "That is the question, is it not? Whether or not you care for her, whether or not you care for her enough to claim her as your own? Here? Now?"

Staring at his brother, Leopold shook his head. "You are mad!" As much as he longed to do as his brother suggested, Leopold knew there were rules, rules he had observed his entire life. "I cannot simply break their engagement. She would be ruined. It is simply not d-"

"But she is not engaged-yet!" Oliver insisted, eagerness upon his face as though breaking rules was as dear to him as upholding them was to Leopold. "You could run off to Gretna Green."

Leopold was about to object—after all, it was an outrageous thought—however, the thought of making Maryann his wife was most tantalizing. Again, his rational mind objected, not simply because it would go against all of society's rules, but also because... Could he truly be certain how he felt? And what about her? "She chose him," he finally said, feeling his heart sink.

Frederick frowned. "Are you saying she does not care for you as you care for her?"

Remembering the few moments they had shared, Leopold could not shake the feeling that she, too, wished for a future with him. He might be deceiving himself because of his own desires; however, the look in her eyes and the slight hitch in her voice he remembered only too well. "I do think she cares for me," he whispered, his gaze distant, his thoughts drawn back to a night a few days ago. "She said she didn't have a choice. She didn't explain but I *know* that she chose Lord Hefferton for other reasons than love."

Frederick moved closer, his gaze thoughtful. "Do you know what these reasons are?"

Leopold shook his head. "I wish I did."

"I might," Kenneth muttered as he stepped forward, the look in his eyes one of serious contemplation.

All eyes turned to him. "Then share what you know!" Oliver demanded in a rush, eagerness upon his face, as though his friend's answer would alter his own fate.

Clearing his throat, Kenneth looked about at the many people moving around them, clearly uncomfortable to speak of another's business. "As far as I know," he began in a hushed voice, "her family is impoverished. Her father was the second son, who did what he could to manage the family's estate when his elder brother inherited the title of baron."

Leopold frowned. "Why did the baron not handle his own affairs?"

Kenneth's voice dropped to a new low, and they all leaned closer to hear him. "He was a drunkard and a gambler, and soon the estate was deep in debt. I heard that her father did what he could to prevent the worst; however, his hands were tied. After his brother passed on and he inherited his father's title, he did his best to repay all debts."

Rolling his eyes, Oliver snorted, "Let me guess, it was an impossibly high sum by then?"

Kenneth nodded. "As far as I know, they are decent people who have suffered a great misfortune." He looked at Leopold. "They need funds, or they will lose everything."

"Do you think her parents are pressuring her into marriage?" Frederick asked, his gaze returning to his brother. "To cover their debts?"

Leopold shrugged, overwhelmed by all that he had heard. He finally knew the burden that rested upon Maryann's shoulders, and it was a heavy one indeed. "That I cannot say." He sighed, "Frankly, we've barely spoken to one another. I know less about her than I know about any of you."

Oliver chuckled, "That is not surprising; after all, you've known us for years." He grinned. "Memorable years."

Ignoring his friend, Frederick stepped in front of Leopold, his hands coming to rest upon his brother's shoulders. "Forget the circumstances," he told him, his gaze insistent as Leopold had never seen it in his carefree brother. "Whatever stands in your way, I'm certain we can find a solution. But the question you must answer for yourself first is, what do you want? How important is she to you?" He glanced sideways to where Lord Hefferton was just now leading Maryann off the dance floor. "Do you want to marry her?"

Leopold stared at Maryann, her gaze meeting his for a split second before she dropped her chin once more, unable to look at him. Did that mean she felt as he did?

"Answer me," Frederick insisted, his hands tightening on Leopold's shoulders. "This is not a moment to dwell on arguments for and against. This is a moment to listen to your blood. What does it tell you?"

Leopold turned to look at his brother. "I...I only met her once before." It would seem that despite all he had felt these past few days, his mind refused to abandon him, to abandon all rational thought, to allow him to choose a new path.

Frederick chuckled, a wide grin upon his face, "Sometimes that's all it takes."

Chapter Eight

TORTURE

A fter escaping Lord Hefferton's company, Maryann sneaked out
onto the terrace, by now in an almost desperate need to clear
her head and breathe in some fresh air. Guilt rested heavily
upon her shoulders, and a dull throbbing had started behind her
temples. Tears still lingered, and at any moment, Maryann feared she
would break down. How had this happened? Only a sennight ago, her
heart had been nowhere near such danger. She had been saddened by
the choice forced upon her by circumstance, angry and disappointed
perhaps, but not heartbroken.

"Are you all right?"

The sound of Leopold's voice sent a shockwave through her.
Maryann whirled around, and in the instant her eyes fell on him, the
dam broke and tears began streaming down her face.

Seeing her reaction, he stilled, his jaw hardening. Then he suddenly
stormed toward her, his hands reaching for hers. "Come with me," he
whispered as his hand took hold of hers, swiftly pulling her off to the
side.

Overcome, Maryann followed him without thought, allowing him
to urge her back against the wall where they would be shielded from
prying eyes. She felt the cool stone wall against her back and looked up

to find Leopold's warm body towering in front of her. Urgency rested in his gaze, but the way he looked at her made her feel precious and safe...at least for a moment.

"Are you all right?" he asked once again, his hand rising to grasp her chin.

Maryann tensed and pulled back the moment the tips of his fingers brushed over her skin. She looked up at him with tearful eyes, feeling her resolve waver. "You must not!" She told him vehemently, afraid that if she did not, all would be lost. "You should not be here. If we are found together, all will be ruined, all I have done will have been for nothing."

His gaze hardened, his jaw set in determination. He allowed her the space she demanded, but he did not move away. "What frightens you so?" His warm gaze once more swept over her face. "I can see how terrified you are. You spoke to me of choices taken out of your hands, of being forced down a path not of your choosing." He inhaled a slow breath, still watching her carefully. "Why did you choose Hefferton? Why is it so important for you to marry him? For that is the plan you speak of, is it not? The plan that might be ruined if we are found together. Am I not right?"

Shocked to hear him uttering these words, Maryann stared up at him, her vision slowly blurring as more tears found their way down her cheeks. Incredible sadness weighed on her heart, and yet, the words to express it failed her, lodged in her throat. "You have no right to speak to me of this," she insisted before her voice all but failed her. "I need to go. I need to return before-" She made to slip past him, but before she had taken more than a single step, his hands once more settled upon her upper arms as they had that night when they had first met.

Stepping in her path, Leopold pulled her back, pressing her against the wall shielding them. His hands felt hot upon her skin, his gaze narrowing, his eyes blazing, as he moved closer. "I will not let you go without words," he hissed, his warm breath fanning over her lips. "I deserve an explanation." He inhaled a slow breath, no more than a sigh. "Perhaps I already know it."

Blinking away her tears, Maryann looked up at him. "Then why do you ask? Why do you insist on prolonging this torture?" Her body trembled in his embrace, and yet, she wished he would hold onto her forever.

His lips thinned. "Torture?" he demanded in a snarl, anger blazing in his eyes. "Does this feel like torture?"

A sob caught in her throat. "Yes," she whispered. "How can it not be? How can I marry Hefferton now, remembering how it felt when you held me?"

Instantly, the expression upon his face softened, becoming warm and reciprocating. His gaze darkened with something unspoken, and he leaned closer, his gaze dropping from hers for a brief second. "What do you feel when I hold you?" he whispered against her lips. "Do you feel unhinged? Do you feel as though someone has lit a fire inside your heart? Do you feel as though you could fly?" He leaned closer, and his forehead came to rest against hers. "Do you feel at peace? Perfectly at peace, and yet, your pulse is thudding so wildly that you fear your heart might stop?"

Maryann closed her eyes, breathing in the scent of him. He was so close, so warm. Never would she forget this moment in his arms. "I do," she whispered, her voice all but gone, her answer no more than a breath.

For a small eternity, they stood like this, their bodies touching, his arms around her, their breaths mingling. Maryann could have remained in this moment forever, or at least she thought so before Leopold's hand once more moved to grasp her chin, tilting it upward, deepest longing in his eyes.

In that moment, when they gazed into each other's eyes, Maryann suddenly wanted more; and as though Leopold had read her thoughts, he bent down and kissed her.

His hand slipped into her hair, holding her to him as his lips brushed against hers, first tentatively and then with more ardour. Maryann melted into his embrace, all thoughts fleeing her mind as she acted on her desire to be close to him, to feel him, to experience this wonder. Indeed, she felt as though she were flying, high in the sky, soaring through the heavens!

Leopold's touch grew from a tentative greeting to a passionate exploration. His hands skimmed over her shoulders, up and down her arms before settling on her waist, pulling her against him. A low growl escaped his throat, and a fierce possessiveness came to his touch.

Maryann felt a curl tumble down her temple as his hands all but raked through her hair, then cupped her face with utter sweetness. She tried to move closer, consumed by the need to feel him, and yet, there was no room left between them, her belly pressed to his, his arms holding her tightly. It was a perfect moment...

...and then footsteps echoed to her ears, dim and as though coming from far away. Still, the sound was like a jolt, and Maryann's eyes jerked open, panic flooding her heart. She pulled away, goose bumps chasing themselves down her arms. "Oh, no."

Looking down at her, Leopold put a warning finger to his lips, urging her to be quiet. Then he leaned to the side, slowly, very slowly, until he was able to peek around the corner. He stilled then, and his gaze narrowed, a hint of contemplation coming to his gaze.

"Maryann?"

Hearing her mother's voice echo to her ears, Maryann jerked anew for she knew, beyond the shadow of a doubt, that if her mother were to find her here, if she saw them together and knew her daughter's heart, she would never allow her to marry Lord Hefferton.

Quickly brushing the curl back behind her ear, Maryann straightened quickly, running her hands over her skirts, then wiped the tears from her eyes and cheeks. She met Leopold's questioning gaze and put a finger to her lips as he had done a moment earlier.

His lips parted as though he wished to ask a question, but Maryann shook her head, then turned away and stepped around him. Inhaling a deep breath, she stepped out of the corner, which had hidden them from her mother's view. She willed a smile onto her face and hoped it looked genuine. "Mother? Is that you?"

Her mother turned around, her gaze narrowing ever so slightly. "There you are, my dear," she exclaimed, hurrying toward her. "I've been looking for you."

Meeting in the middle of the terrace, Maryann moved to step around her mother so that she herself was the one to look in the direction of the hidden corner where Leopold still hid. "I've simply been enjoying the fresh air," Maryann told her mother, willing her eyes not to stray to the hiding place she knew was there. "Is there something you wish to speak to me about?"

Holding her daughter's gaze, the baroness inhaled a slow breath as though needing to gather her courage for what she was about to say. Maryann felt an ice-cold shiver run down her spine. "Indeed, there is," her mother stated, her jaw slightly tense, revealing a hint of disapproval. "It would seem Lord Hefferton invited your father to join him in his study."

Maryann tensed. "In his study? But why?"

Her mother reached out and grasped her daughter's hands. "They signed the contract," she told her daughter with watchful eyes. "It would seem you are finally betrothed." Her mother's gaze searched her face, and Maryann fought to maintain her composure when in truth she felt like crumbling to the ground into a weeping mess. "Are you all right, dear? This is what you wanted, is it not?"

Maryann swallowed, her cheeks aching from the strain of smiling. "Of course, it is. You know that, Mother. I... I am most overjoyed."

Her mother nodded; still, doubt remained in her eyes. "I believe your betrothed intends to announce your engagement within a fortnight."

Still smiling, Maryann nodded. "Very well. That suits me."

"A busy time is ahead of us," her mother commented, a puff of air escaping her lips as her eyes turned heavenward in thought. "A wedding to suit Lord Hefferton's expectations will not be an easy feat. A lot will be required of us in the coming weeks. Are you up for that?"

Maryann nodded; it seemed she was incapable of anything else. "Certainly, Mother." She clenched her hands as they began to tremble, and panic slowly crawled up her skin. "Will you...will you give me a moment? I admit, this news is quite overwhelming after all. I could do with a moment alone."

Her mother smiled at her gently, then brushed her hand over her cheek, frowning slightly when she felt a hint of wetness upon Maryann's skin. "Of course, darling. Take all the time you need." Then she returned inside.

The second the doors closed behind her mother, Maryann's knees buckled, and she collapsed on the hard terrace floor.

Chapter Nine

SHOULD AND SHOULDN'T

Leopold's insides churned. It felt as though a hot coal rested in his belly, burning its way through him. He remained hidden behind the stone wall corner, his hands balled into fists and his feet eager to rush out.

Always had he been a rational man, not one prone to fits of anger or rash actions. He tended to think things through thoroughly before acting, quite unlike his younger brother, who often rushed headfirst into the unknown. However, here, in this moment, Leopold wanted nothing more than to barrel out into the open and claim Maryann for himself.

Doubts had been with him before; nevertheless, hearing her mother announce Maryann's engagement to another had changed all that. In the moment, she was completely lost to him; he knew without question that she was the one.

That he wanted her.

That he could not let her go.

That he loved her.

His heart ached so fiercely that he thought it would give out any moment. Pain radiated from it into every region of his body. It felt crippling, devastating, lethal. The only small consolation was the look upon Maryann's face for it told him clear as day that she felt as he did. This news was not good news for her; in fact, she looked all but destroyed.

A few more words were exchanged between mother and daughter before the elder woman headed back inside. The moment she disappeared from view, Leopold noticed a change in Maryann.

All of a sudden, she seemed vulnerable, weak, barely able to hold herself upright. All strength had left her, her iron will no longer able to fool her body.

In the next moment, her eyes closed, a look of exhaustion upon her face, and Leopold knew what was about to happen.

Without thought for discovery, he surged forward in the very moment her legs buckled. She slumped downward, and his heart jumped into his throat.

Leopold all but threw himself forward and barely managed to catch her before she hit the ground. His breath came fast as she fell into his arms, her body limp. "Maryann?" he called as loud as he dared.

Her eyelids began to flutter, and then she was looking up at him. "Leopold?" she whispered, and his name upon her lips brought him unexpected joy. "What happened?"

With a glance in the direction of the windows, behind which Lord Hefferton's guests were still dancing and chatting, Leopold pushed himself back onto his feet, hoisting her in his arms. Then in a few quick steps, they were back in their hidden corner.

He could only hope no one had seen them.

Gently, he set her down upon her feet, her hands holding onto him to steady herself. Leopold could not help but smile for it reminded him of the night they had met when *he* had been the one in need of support.

Her wide eyes looked up at him, her fingers still curled into his jacket. "What happened?" She asked again, her gaze drifting to the side, to where she had collapsed a moment ago. "Mother...she...I..." Then her eyes suddenly widened, growing as round as plates.

Leopold exhaled the breath he had been holding, his arms still locking her in a tight embrace. "Do you remember what happened?

Maryann swallowed, then nodded. "She told me I..." Her voice broke off, and he could see a slight tremor in her jaw. Tears once again pulled in her eyes. "You saw? And heard?"

Leopold nodded. "I did," he forced out through gritted teeth. "It would seem you are finally engaged." There was a bite in his voice that she did not deserve, but one he could not prevent for the news had hurt him as much as her.

She closed her eyes, and her head sank.

Instantly, Leopold felt awful. What had happened had not been her choice; she had made that clear from the beginning. "What do you want?" he asked her, yet again grasping her chin and making her look up at him. "Aside from all you think you *should* do, what is it you want?"

A lone tear snaked its way down her cheek. "Do not ask me that," she sobbed, her head shaking from side to side ever so slightly. "Please, do not ask me that."

"I must!" Leopold hissed, barely able to contain his fury, his desperation, that sense of doom that lingered. "Because I love you." He had not meant to hurl these words into her face, but they needed to be said.

She needed to hear them.

Staring up at him, Maryann stilled. Her jaw dropped, and her breath came in panting gasps.

"I love you," he repeated more gently, his hand moving from her chin and rising to cup her face, "and I want you as my wife." It was a bittersweet moment as they stood there in each other's embrace; their eyes locked, hope lingering in the air.

Then, however, Maryann began to shake her head, fear suddenly etched into her eyes. "No! No! No! You cannot! You must not!"

Leopold tensed, holding onto her even more tightly as she threatened to slip away. "You can shake your head as much as you like, it will not change the truth." When she tried to turn her head away, he once more grasped her chin. "Do you deny that you care for me?"

More tears welled up in her eyes. "It does not matter what I feel or what you feel," she sobbed. "I told you before that this was not my choice, and that has not changed. Please, do not make this any harder."

"Do not for a second believe I will simply let you slip away."

Leopold leaned closer, feeling her warm breath upon his skin. "Why do you insist on this marriage? Is it your parents? Do they pressure you?"

At his words, her jaw set in determination. "My parents are the kindest, most caring people I have ever known," she told him with such devotion that he could not doubt her words. "There are circumstances you know nothing about, circumstances I cannot change; but I can ensure that my family is taken care off. All my life, my parents have seen to my happiness. Now, it is my turn to see to theirs."

Remembering what Kenneth had told them, Leopold began to understand. "If the only reason for you to marry Hefferton is your concern for your parents," he whispered gently, "then marry me instead, and I swear I will see to all of you."

For a long moment, Maryann stared at him. He could see a spark of temptation in her eyes. Whether it had truly been there or not, Leopold did not know, but he liked to believe so. Then, however, she once more shook her head. "I cannot," she gasped as though shocked by her own reply. "I gave my word. My father gave his. A contract was signed."

"Then let us run away together," Leopold heard himself suggest, echoing Oliver's earlier thought. It surprised him as much as her, and yet, he could not regret uttering it.

Lifting her hands, Maryann pushed against his chest, trying to free herself from his tight grip. "Please, release me. You cannot mean what you say. It is madness!"

Reluctantly, Leopold dropped his arms and took a step back. "What is madness," he said as calmly as he could, "is for us to go separate ways. Do you want that?" He searched her eyes. "Be certain you know what you want because the choice you make now will affect the rest of your life." He swallowed hard. "As well as mine."

With her hands braced against the rough stone wall, Maryann stood there, her eyes wide and full of tears as she looked at him. Moments ticked by; one by one. Then, slowly, she inhaled a deep breath, the look in her eyes changing, growing harder, and he knew that she had come to a decision. "You are the most wonderful man I have ever met," she whispered through a curtain of tears as she stepped forward, her palms coming to rest upon his chest. "I shall never forget you." The moment the last word had left her lips, she pushed closer and brushed a quick kiss against his lips. Then she darted off, leaving him behind, alone and heartbroken.

Unable to move his feet, Leopold all but sagged back against the wall, feeling the rough stone through the layers of fabric he wore. His eyes closed as a feeling of deep hopelessness washed over him. How had this happened? A week ago, he had never even met her, and now she was the very life of him. Again, his parent's words echoed in his head telling him that he would know, simply know, when he had found the one he was meant to be with.

And he did know.

Leopold knew without even the barest of doubts, and yet, it did not matter.

"Leo?"

Hearing his brother call for him, Leopold reluctantly pushed off from the wall and stepped out of the hiding place he had shared with Maryann. "I'm here."

Whirling around, Frederick instantly started toward him, but stopped the second his gaze fell on Leopold's face. "She refused you?" He shook his head, stepping closer, grasping his brother's arm and pulling him aside. "What happened?"

It was agony to speak to his brother about the loss he had just suffered for speaking the words seemed to make it more real, more final. "All is lost."

Frederick grasped his shoulder, squeezing it hard. "Why would you say that? Why would you give up so easily? Do you not know that the things worth fighting for are the hardest to obtain?"

The seriousness in his brother's voice teased a small smile onto Leopold's face. "How would you know that, Brother? Have you ever found yourself in such a situation?"

Frederick shook his head. "I have not," he admitted. "But neither am I blind. I have eyes, and I can see exactly how much she means to you. You look at her as Father looks at Mother, and I know that you need her by your side."

Leopold sighed, his body suddenly feeling exhausted. "It seems it does not matter."

Frederick's brows drew down into an angry frown. "Do you need me to slap you?" he asked, his voice dark and challenging. "You know as well as I do why she refused you. She—"

"Why would it matter why she refused me? The result is the same."

Frederick glared at him. "Have you always been one to give up so easily?" he asked, open disapproval in his voice. "Contracts can be changed. Engagements can be dissolved. Even if Lord Hefferton were to sue her parents for breach of contract, why should it matter? If you marry her, her problems will be yours, and I have no doubt that Father will see to everything."

Indeed, the thought had occurred to Leopold, and yet, it felt wrong. Certainly, his family could afford to buy their way out of the contract. Their influence was great, and Leopold knew as well as his brother that his father would find a way to pacify Lord Hefferton. But if they did so, would he not have bought her? Would he not have used his money, like Hefferton, to gain her hand?

"There has to be another way," Leopold said, breathing in a deep breath, willing himself to ignore the exhaustion that had been lingering in his body these past few moments. "There must be another way."

His brother grinned at him. "Now, that's the spirit," Frederick exclaimed, approval now marking his features. "Always have you been so serious, aware of the rules and how the world works. If anyone can find a way out of the situation, it is you."

Nodding to his brother, Leopold stepped away, moving up to the balustrade, his gaze fixed out into the gardens. Thoughts ran rampant in his head, from side to side, in circles; thoughts that could only be described as madness, but they led him onward. And slowly, very slowly, the thoughts in his mind began to make sense.

Leopold lifted his chin and turned to his brother. "In order to see to her family's debts," he began, carefully connecting each thought with the next, "I believe a lucrative business venture could be a solution. I have friends, who are quite knowledgeable in these matters. I shall write to them immediately."

Frederick nodded approvingly, the smile upon his face growing wider. "What about Hefferton?"

The man's name sent a jolt of jealousy through Leopold's heart.

The thought that one day soon he could be Maryann's husband nearly destroyed him; but he had to keep his wits. He needed to think... clearly. "There has to be a reason—of course, there is—why he chose her." His teeth gritted together. "Is he in love with her?" Of course, the thought was not unreasonable; yet, Leopold hoped with every fibre of his being that it was not so because from personal experience he now knew that Hefferton would never release her if he loved her.

"Then we shall find out," Frederick declared, already taking a step back towards the French doors leading into the ballroom. "Leave it to me. I shall find out what you need to know."

And then he was gone, and once again Leopold remained behind, his thoughts drawn to the only woman who had ever stolen his heart. Admittedly, he knew very little about her; however, he knew from what she had told him, from the way she had spoken to him that he could not simply go over her head in this matter; at least, not where her word was concerned. She was an honourable, loyal woman, and she would never dream of treating Lord Hefferton with anything less than respect, no matter what it would cost her.

"There has to be a way to dissuade him from this marriage," Leopold mumbled to himself as he stood in front of the glass doors and watched his brother address his friends across the ballroom.

Chapter Ten

THE COUNSEL OF FRIENDS

Not a word passed between them as Maryann and Leonora walked side-by-side through Hyde Park. The sun was shining, and a mild breeze stirred the leaves. Children ran laughing across the lawns; in the distance, the clear waters of the Serpentine sparkled in the afternoon sun.

Biting her lower lip, Maryann cast a careful glance at her companion, words eager to escape her lips; however, caution held her back.

Birds sang in the trees to their right as the two women walked another few steps in silence, their maids trailing a good distance behind them.

"It is a beautiful day, is it not?" Leonora remarked, with another sideways glance.

Maryann nodded. "It is indeed."

On they walked, proceeding down a bend in the path, nature sounds all that echoed between them.

Maryann's fingers fidgeted with a handkerchief she held, its edges now tattered, proof of the tumult in her head and heart. More words seemed to claw their way up her throat, pushing to be released into the world, to be heard. She gritted her teeth, knowing she should not speak what was on her mind. Why then, however, had she invited Leonora out for a stroll? If not to speak to her?

Emotions warred within her; then, a few steps farther down the path, the dam finally broke. Pulling to an abrupt halt, Maryann whirled around, grasped Leonora's hands tightly, and staring at the other woman with wide eyes blurted out, "I do not love the man I'm supposed to marry." Equal measures of shock and relief flooded her being, and her breath rushed from her lungs in a sharp gust.

For a moment, Leonora simply stared at her, too overcome to respond. Then, however, a soft smile slowly claimed the young woman's face, her hands gently squeezing Maryann's in return. "I do not love my husband," she admitted, balancing the scales between them. "At least, not the way I should, not the way he deserves."

Maryann nodded. "My betrothed is a good man. He deserves a wife who cares for him, who has not given her heart to another."

"My husband is a wonderful father," Leonora reciprocated, tears shining in her blue eyes. "He loves our daughter with all his heart, and I love him for it." A shuddering breath escaped her. "I wish I could give him more, but another holds my heart."

Both women looked at one another with tearful eyes, then sank into each other's arms, silently sobbing for the love they had lost or were about to lose. "We are a pair, are we not?" Leonora chuckled, then pulled back, wiping at her tears.

Maryann nodded. "But it feels good to say it out loud to one who can understand."

Leonora agreed. "May I ask," she began carefully, a question in her eyes, "why did you agree to marry him?"

"My family needs the connection," Maryann admitted, feeling as though a block of ice were settling in her stomach. "We are greatly in debt, and there is no other way out of it." It was an embarrassing admission, and yet, it had not been their fault. They had done the best they could, but it had not been enough.

"And the man you love," Leonora inquired, "he is not of your station? You could not marry him instead?"

Maryann stilled, her eyes becoming distant, for only in this very moment did she realize that Leopold was indeed a viable alternative. It was a revolting thought, though, because she loved him and did not wish to see him as a solution to her problem. "It is too late now for regrets," she told Leonora instead. "Contracts have been signed. It is done."

Leonora nodded, a shadow passing over her face. "Yes, there are always reasons, circumstances outside of our control. Sometimes no matter how hard we wish for something, it is simply unattainable." She blinked back fresh tears, and once again squeezed Maryann's hands. "Let us take comfort in each other for it is all we have."

"Thank you," Maryann whispered, grateful to have finally found a friend she could confide in. "I am glad I stepped on your foot the other night." A soft chuckle rumbled in her throat, and the corners of her mouth quirked upward. "Indeed, I am most grateful."

Leonora smiled at her. "As am I, my friend. As am I."

Leopold rarely paced, but right now he was pacing. His mind was running in circles, never arriving anywhere. He did not know what to do, and he had hoped that speaking to his parents might help him come to the right decision. Unfortunately, they could not persuade the earth to change its rotation either. They could not move mountains nor drain the seas. They supported him, had told him that whatever decision he would make, they would stand by his side. They were his parents, and they wanted to see him happy, but they could not change the world for him.

Leopold had known that even before he had spoken to them. Still, it had felt good to hear their unconditional support. Leopold loved his parents dearly, as much as Maryann loved her own, he suspected. The way she spoke of them, the lengths she was willing to go to to protect them was proof of a deep bond. No matter what decision Leopold would come to, he knew he needed to be mindful of that. A decision that would harm her parents in any way would not be one Maryann would approve of.

And so, Leopold continued to pace up and down the path cutting through the gardens of his parent's townhouse. The gravel crunched beneath his boots, and the birds twittered in his ears. He felt a soft breeze whistle through the leaves overhead and wished the wind could whisper to him of what he ought to do. He could not allow Maryann to marry Hefferton, but neither could he ruin her in an effort to secure her hand. Neither option was truly an option. What was he to do?

"You look like a madman!"

At his brother's charming comparison, Leopold's head snapped up. He whirled around, hoping against hope that somehow Frederick had found a solution, a solution that eluded him.

With a wide grin upon his face, Frederick strode over to him, his two childhood friends Kenneth and Oliver by his side.

A little father up the path, Leopold spotted Charlotte, a family friend of Kenneth's. She was young and not out in society, but her hazel eyes were watchful and curious as always as she followed Kenneth wherever he went. It had always been thus, ever since they had been little children.

As the men proceeded onward, Charlotte stayed behind by the rosebushes, occasionally glancing in their direction, her open gaze as curious as ever.

"Any ideas?" Leopold wrung his hands as he looked from his brother to his friends.

Leopold's heart sank when he saw his brother's smile fade a little. "No new ones," Frederick replied, with a sigh. "However, I do believe the old ones should be revisited."

Disappointed, Leopold shook his head. "I cannot do that to her. She would never forgive me." Once again, his gaze moved from Frederick to Oliver and then to Kenneth. "What did you find out? What kind of man is Hefferton? Does he...love her?"

"He seems to fancy her," Oliver remarked with a shrug, glancing a bit uncertainly at Kenneth. "I do not believe it to be love though."

Kenneth nodded in agreement.

Leopold breathed a sigh of relief. "Do you think he could be persuaded to give her up?"

Frederick shrugged, taking a step toward him. "I suppose, should he see you with her..." He grinned devilishly.

Leopold shook his head. "I will not agree to anything that will bring shame to her family." His gaze hardened as he looked at his brother. "Let's not revisit that particular idea again. Any others?" His hands began to tremble as he felt a sense of inevitability fall over him. He kept asking the same questions, hoping for new answers, but there simply were none.

With a sideways glance at his friends, Kenneth stepped forward, a look of understanding in his gaze as he met Leopold's eyes. "I'm afraid there is not much I can tell you," he said, an apologetic look upon his face. "Indeed, Lord Hefferton seems to be a kind man, who is coming to care for Miss Hayes. He treats her in the most respectful manner as he does everybody else. His reputation is utterly untainted. He is a man of honour." Kenneth exhaled a slow breath, no doubt knowing full well what his words meant to Leopold. "He would never break his word once given."

Raking his hands through his hair, Leopold spun around and began to pace once more, up and down a short stretch of the path. "What then?" He looked up at them, then stopped. "Why her? Why did he choose her? Why not another if it is not love?"

Frederick stepped forward. "The man requires neither funds nor title for he possesses both. As far as we were able to find out what he cherishes most is his family's honour and reputation." Frederick chuckled, "It is so clean it might not be unreasonable to assume you could see your own reflection in it."

Frederick frowned. "So, you think he chose her because he believes...?" He paused, looking from one man to the other.

Kenneth nodded. "It is a reasonable assumption. Her manners are impeccable, and aside from her uncle's reputation, the family is highly esteemed in upper circles. The blame falls to the late baron; whereas, most people highly approve of the way his younger brother, Maryann's father, has conducted himself."

"So, it seems," Oliver threw in with a bit of an eye roll, "that the man does not hold her family's mistakes against her. I expect, short of ruining her, there is nothing you can do to dissuade him from marrying her."

Leopold could have groaned. The situation was as bad as he had expected. Never in his life had he hoped to be wrong. Never in his life had he felt more disappointed.

Frederick frowned. "Will you truly take a step back and let her do this? Yes, she might be angry with you, but in the end, she will be your wife. Her anger will fade and she will forgive you, do you not believe so?"

Leopold closed his eyes, a part of him thinking as his brother did. "She might," he whispered as the wind brushed through his hair. "But what if she doesn't? It is no foundation to build a good marriage upon. I want her to *want* to be my wife. I don't want to go behind her back or over her head. I want to make this decision *with* her, not *for* her," his head sank, "and she has made it perfectly clear that she will not sacrifice her parent's happiness for her own. I must respect her decision."

Oliver and Frederick exchanged disbelieving looks, then Frederick charged forward grasping Leopold by the shoulders. "This is madness!" he snapped. "You will truly stand by and watch her marry another man? Are you a fool?" He shook his head. "Speak to her again. Make her see reason."

Leopold shrugged off his brother's hands, taking a step back as anger began to swirl in his blood. "Don't you think I want to? Do you honestly believe I make this decision lightly?" Once again, he raked his hand through his hair, feeling a sharp tug upon his skin. "There is no reason; no reason that would persuade her to change her mind. She does what she does out of love. She's being selfless, how can I be any less so?"

Rubbing his hand over his face, Frederick seemed to be grasping for words. "But she wants to marry you," he pointed out harshly. "If her father had not signed the contract, she –"

"But he did!" Leopold replied with equal vehemence. "He did. The contract is signed, and to her that is binding. She will not go back on her word. She will not dishonour her family." He sighed, "That is the woman she is, and I admire that about her."

All four men fell silent, staring at one another, torn between defeat and the hope that in the last moment one of them might come up with a magical solution.

"Pardon me?" A soft, barely audible voice spoke out from behind Kenneth's shoulder. They all flinched at the sudden interruption of the lingering stillness and spun around to find Charlotte standing there, a bit of a sheepish grin upon her face as she wrung her hands.

"Did I not ask you to stay behind?" Kenneth addressed her gently, only a mild rebuke in his voice as he stepped forward and reached for her hands. "We have something rather important to discuss." His demeanour was that of an elder brother, torn between indulging his little sister and walking his own way, without her shadowing him.

She nodded. "I understand," Charlotte whispered, her wide hazel eyes slowly drifting to Leopold. "But I have an idea." Again, she looked at Kenneth for approval. "I apologize for eavesdropping, but please hear me out. Please."

Leopold felt his heart stop as hope once more sent a jolt through it. "What is your idea?" he asked, stepping towards her.

Charlotte cast Kenneth a small smile, then approached Leopold. "From what I overheard," again she grinned sheepishly, "I understand that ruining Miss Hayes – is it? – would not sit well with the lady; understandably." She looked over her shoulder at Kenneth, who seemed rather tense at the thought that Charlotte had gotten involved in this matter. "Perhaps what you should do is find a convincing way to point out to Lord Hefferton that Miss Hayes is not the bride he is looking for," she said, carefully choosing her words, occasionally glancing over her shoulder at Kenneth. "Perhaps something more private would suffice, something only for Lord Hefferton's attention. If done right, no one else would ever have to find out. I'm certain as Lord Hefferton is a most respectable gentleman, he would not breathe a word of anything untoward to another; also, it would implicate his own connection to her."

For a stunned moment, all four men remained quiet. Then Oliver slapped his knee, a wide grin spreading over his face. "This is genius, Charlotte!"

Leopold tensed, afraid to hope again, only to be disappointed again. "How so?" He asked. "How can we possibly...?"

Frederick grasped his shoulder, his anger replaced by enthusiasm. "Oh, big brother, there is always a way." He met Oliver's gaze, and both men nodded to each other, clearly a plan was already forming in their minds. But what kind of plan? How would it be different from the one they had already proposed? "Leave it to us," Frederick said with an even wider grin, quickly rushing on when he saw Leopold was about to object, "I promise, no harm shall come to her family. You have my word."

Leopold inhaled a deep breath, his gaze holding his brother's. Never had Frederick betrayed him in any way. He was wild and reckless sometimes, but he was a good man, a man of his word, and Leopold trusted him. "Very well," he said, allowing the beginnings of a smile to form on his face. "I hope you know what you're doing. For both our sakes."

Frederick chuckled. "I rarely do, but fortunately for me, you have no other option. I'm all you've got." Then he drew Leopold into a quick embrace before spinning around and hurrying off with Oliver, their heads bent toward one another, whispering. Leopold could only hope that all would end well.

Turning, he looked at Charlotte. "Thank you for your thoughts."

Slinking her arm through Kenneth's, Charlotte smiled at him. "I only hope it will work, but it must. Do you not believe so?" She looked up at Kenneth with trusting eyes. "Love should always triumph; should it not?"

Leopold agreed wholeheartedly; but he knew that life could be harsh sometimes. He could only hope that this was not one of those times.

Chapter Eleven

TRUST ME

" If it is agreeable to you," Lord Hefferton addressed Maryann during a minuet, "we shall announce our engagement in a few days." He smiled at her kindly.

Holding onto her own smile, Maryann nodded. "Of course, my lord." After all, there was no sense in delaying the inevitable, was there?

Still, sadness settled in her heart at the thought of her impending nuptials. It ought not be thus, ought it? She ought to feel joyful and expectant, not this, not this gloom or dread. After all, the man she would marry was a truly kind man. He deserved to be happy, but did she not also? Why could they not find happiness together? It might have been possible before she had met Leopold, but now Maryann knew that her heart would never love another.

After the dance ended, Leonora suddenly appeared by their side. "Pardon me, my lord," she addressed Lord Hefferton with a bewitching smile, "but I must steal Miss Hayes from you for a short moment. It is most important."

Confused, Maryann frowned at her new friend.

"Of course," her betrothed agreed, a warm smile upon his face as he turned to her. "I shall see you shortly," his voice dropped slightly, "my dear." Then he stepped back, bowed his head to them and walked away.

"Come with me," Leonora urged as she grasped Maryann's hand and pulled her forward through the crowd.

Not being given a choice, Maryann followed. "What is going on? Where are we going?"

"It is a surprise," Leonora whispered over her shoulder as they left behind the ballroom and disappeared down a long corridor. Their footsteps were swallowed up by the heavy rug running down its length. "This way." Leonora drew to a halt and threw open a door, leading into a darkened room. Once inside, she spun around, a big smile upon her face as she looked at Maryann. "Wait here," she instructed before making to step away.

Maryann tensed, reaching out to stop her. "Where are you going? You cannot leave me here on my own. What if–?"

Turning back to her, Leonora grasped Maryann's hands, a look of joyful expectation upon her lovely face. "Trust me," she whispered, the hint of tears in her eyes. "I'm doing this so you will have your happily-ever-after after all. You deserve it, and this is your only chance."

Maryann felt a cold shiver dance down her spine, mingling with the sudden warmth shooting through her heart. "But–"

Leonora shook her head. "Do not question this," she said, squeezing Maryann's hands. "Trust me when I say that all will be well." Then she stepped back, her hands releasing Maryann's, and moved to the door. "Wait here." And in the next moment, she was gone.

Maryann remained behind, alone, staring at the closed door. Her thoughts were running rampant, trying their best to analyse what Leonora had said as well as all possible meanings. Goosebumps broke out all over her skin, and she lifted her hands to rub them up and down her arms. Her nerves were in a jumble, and she began shifting from one foot onto the other nervously.

And then the door suddenly opened...and Maryann went still.

To her utter shock, it was none other than Leopold who stepped inside. His brown eyes shone with warmth and affection, and his hands reached for hers longingly. His skin felt almost hot compared to her own chilled fingers, and she instantly moved toward him. It felt as though an old instinct propelled her into his arms, her eyes wide as she gazed up at him, a smile claiming her features, one that had been absent for far too long. "What are you doing here? You shouldn't... We shouldn't..."

A broad smile claimed his face, and he reached up and gently brushed a curl behind her ear, the tips of his fingers grazing her skin. "I know what you said," he whispered, lowering his head to hers, his breath fanning over her lips, "and I assure you that I heard you. However, I cannot simply walk away. If I did, I would regret it for the rest of my life."

Maryann loved these words, but they also frightened her. "What are you saying?"

He swallowed hard, his gaze on hers, no words tumbling from his lips as he looked at her for a long moment. "Trust me. Please, trust me." Then he stepped back, his left hand reaching for hers while his right opened the door. "Come."

Completely at a loss, Maryann followed him back out into the corridor. It lay deserted, and they proceeded onward, turning a corner that led them farther away from the ballroom. "Where are we going?"

"We're almost there," Leopold replied and then suddenly pulled to a halt, turning around to face her.

Not having expected that, Maryann all but ran into his arms.

Leopold caught her swiftly and held her close, his hands settling around her waist. A slow smile lit up his face as she bit her lower lip to keep the corners of her mouth from rising involuntarily upward. But they did, and she could tell from the way his warm brown eyes were looking into hers that this moment meant as much to him as it did to her.

It did.

It was precious and priceless and out of a dream, and yet, it also terrified her. It was not right for them to be here, alone, together. What if someone were to happen upon them? What if her betrothed were to see her in Leopold's arms?

Again, Maryann was of two minds when she contemplated this possibility. A part of her rejoiced while another sunk down in desperation. "I must go," she whispered, trying to pull away, finding it hard to do so. Not only was Leopold refusing to release her, but also because she did not truly wish to go. "What if–?"

"Do not worry," Leopold said, his voice so calm and reassuring that Maryann almost believed him. "Do you trust me?" he asked all of a sudden, his brow slightly drawn into a frown. For a moment, she thought that he was holding his breath, afraid to hear her answer, afraid that she might not.

Brushing a hand over his cheek, Maryann smiled up at him. "I do," she told him joyfully. "Of course, I do. I don't know why, I barely know you, but I do."

The smile that came to his face could have lit up the night; it was dazzling and overwhelming and so beautiful. "Then trust me now," he whispered before his gaze briefly darted to something beyond her shoulder. It lingered there for no more than a second or two before returning to her. "I promise all will be clear in due time."

Feeling puzzled, Maryann was about to ask what he meant when Leopold suddenly turned them sideways. Her feet moved with him to keep her balance, her gaze locked upon his, her brow still drawn into a frown.

And then she felt his hands upon her waist tighten, urging her closer, before a moment later he swept her deeper into his embrace. Maryann barely had time to voice her surprise; no more than a breathy gasp escaped her lips before Leopold sealed them with his own.

The kiss felt heavenly, and Maryann lost herself in it. New sensations sparked everywhere, dancing over her skin and humming deep inside her. She clung to him, her hands touching his face, her fingertips feeling the softness of his skin where his chin dipped down into his neck. She felt his heart beating against her own, skipping a beat alongside with hers. They were like one, and in this perfect moment, Maryann dared believe that they would be for all the days to come.

And then the dream ended when angry footsteps echoed to her ears, the sound slowly fighting its way through the fog that shrouded her in safety and hid her from reality.

Maryann froze, terror reawakening in her heart.

Chapter Twelve

MEN OF HONOUR

Leopold marvelled at the rightness of holding Maryann in his arms. Never before in his life had he been more certain of anything. As shocking as the revelation was, Frederick had been right. Time was nothing. Time did not matter when it came to knowing who he loved. If he had a year to decide, the answer would still be the same.

Her.

She was the one.

Losing himself in the moment, Leopold barely heard the footsteps echoing closer. He forced his mind to focus, to stop lingering on their kiss and recall the plan he had set in motion. He could only hope all would go well, and by the end of the night, she would be his as he was hers already.

Maryann tensed, and he knew in that moment that she too had heard another's approach.

Reluctantly breaking their kiss, Leopold lifted his head. He saw her eyes going wide, a hint of fear etched into them. Her breath came fast, if from the fear of discovery or their kiss he could not say, but he hoped for the latter. "Trust me now," he whispered before he turned away, readying himself to face her betrothed's wrath.

Lord Hefferton was charging down the corridor toward them, his jaw clenched, and his hands balled at his sides. Anger and disappointment stood in his eyes, but Leopold could also see shock and sadness marking his features. Perhaps the man had truly come to care for Maryann. "What is this?" he demanded, his hard stare moving from Leopold to Maryann and back. "How dare you lay a hand on her?"

Behind Leopold, a sob tore from Maryann's lips. "I'm sorry. I'm so, so deeply sorry," she mumbled, her voice faint and full of shock.

Hefferton's gaze softened ever so slightly, and Leopold felt a moment of regret. Indeed, the man was honourable, and he deserved better. In the end, however, that was exactly what he would receive; a new chance with someone who could absolutely love him.

Doing his best to ignore Maryann's misery, Leopold stepped toward Hefferton, his mind focused on the task at hand. "I apologize," he began, fighting to remain calm, "for what you had to witness. However, it was necessary to prove a point."

Hefferton glared at him. "To prove what point?" he gritted out through clenched teeth.

Leopold inhaled a slow breath. "You have a choice to make," he told Hefferton, praying that the other man would see reason and choose right. "I love her," Leopold blurted out, feeling the rightness of his words resonate throughout his whole body.

Hefferton stared at him, thunderstruck.

Leopold merely nodded, then glanced over his shoulder and looked at Maryann, knowing in that moment that she felt as he did. Then he forced himself to turn back around, meeting the other man's gaze once more. "I love her, and she loves me. I intend to marry her. So, you see, your own intentions present a problem. The only solution is for you to dissolve the contract you have signed and set her free."

Hefferton turned a dark shade of red. "How dare you speak to me like this? Do you have no honour, sneaking around behind my back with designs for the woman I am betrothed to?" He shook his head at Leopold as a parent might shake their head at a child who had disappointed them somehow.

Leopold sighed, "I understand your anger," he told the other man. "I assure you I do. But perhaps you can also understand what it feels like to finally meet the woman you love and find her betrothed to another. What would you do if you were in my place? Would you let her marry another and spend the rest of your life wishing you hadn't? Or would you do everything within your power to make her your wife?"

Hefferton's nostrils flared; anger still burned in his eyes Still, Leopold could feel the other man watching him, contemplating his words. "If this becomes known," he said in a surprisingly calm voice, "all our reputations shall suffer. Have you considered that?" He glanced behind Leopold at Maryann.

"I have," Leopold replied, seeing the other man's gaze narrow. "That is why I have set up this little scene right here, right now, out of the way of the assembled guests. Contrary to the way it might seem, we are not alone."

On cue, Lady Kensington stepped out of the shadows and came to stand by Maryann's side, gently taking her hand in hers. Farther up and down the corridor, Frederick, Oliver, and Kenneth made their presence known, standing guard at each entrance that led to the point where they stood.

"You see, no one could have come upon us here unexpectedly." He took a step closer to Lord Hefferton and then lowered his voice. "I would never ruin her," he said quietly, holding the other man's gaze, "in order to claim her hand. All I wanted was for you to see that her heart will never be yours. I am deeply sorry for the pain this realization may cause you, but believe me I am doing you a service by opening your eyes now, by preventing this marriage."

For a long moment, Lord Hefferton remained still, his gaze utterly unrevealing. Then he blinked, looked at Leopold with an oddly intense gaze before stepping around him and toward Maryann.

Allowing them a moment to themselves, Leopold remained with his back to them. He heard Hefferton ask, "Is this truly what you want? Do you no longer wish to be my wife?"

Stillness hung over the corridor as Leopold held his breath. He wanted to look over his shoulder. He wanted to see Maryann's face, to know what her answer would be, but this had to be her decision.

After a small eternity, Maryann finally spoke. "It is," she whispered, a deep sense of shame and regret in her voice. "I am deeply sorry for wounding you thus. I assure you it was never my intention. You are a good and kind man, and perhaps I could have loved you if..." Her voice trailed off. "You deserve better," she added then, more strength now in the way she spoke. "I am not who you want, and I hope with all my heart that one day you will find the woman who will love you as you deserve."

Leopold closed his eyes, savouring the moment. His heart beat fast in his chest, stronger now, encouraged by the knowledge that she loved him and that she had just chosen him out of her own free will.

Wishing to reach a mutually benefiting conclusion, Leopold finally turned around and addressed Lord Hefferton. "What do you say?" he asked the other man, who slowly turned from Maryann and faced him.

His jaw remained tense; however, only little anger remained in his gaze. "Considering how well you have planned all this," he stated with a slight wave of his hand, encompassing the scene they found themselves in, "how do you propose we proceed?"

Leopold inhaled a slow breath, exchanging a quick glance with Maryann. "No one need ever know of your engagement," he told Hefferton. "You and Lord Everleigh can both step back from the contract, and Maryann will be free to marry whom she chooses...as will you."

Sighing, Lord Hefferton nodded. "And what of all the witnesses you have invited to this private moment? What assurance do I have that none shall breathe a word of what happened here tonight?"

"I understand your caution," Leopold assured him. "However, all currently present here hold my utmost confidence and trust or I would not have invited them to join us. I give you my word that nothing shall ever be known of what happened here tonight."

Lord Hefferton nodded. "Very well. If this is what you wish," he glanced at Maryann, "then I shall not stand in your way." He respectfully inclined his head toward her, then took a step back, turned on his heel and marched back the way he had come.

Maryann squeezed Leonora's hand so hard that she felt certain it would fall off any moment now. Her own nerves were tense to the point of breaking as she stared at Lord Hefferton's receding back. Her mind still had trouble understanding all that had happened in the last few moments. She felt joy that her future would now no longer be tied to a man she could not love; however, there was also a great sadness because now once again the future was uncertain, and Maryann worried about her parents and all they had suffered and all they would.

"Are you all right?" Leonora asked her, her blue eyes searching Maryann's. "You're shaking like a leaf." Her gaze moved and she looked over her shoulder. "Lord Bentham?"

Turning to them, Leopold met her gaze, and then in an instant, he was with her. Leonora's hand slipped from Maryann's iron grip, and Leopold's arms encircled her, holding her close. His eyes looked down into hers, and she barely heard Leonora walk away, leaving them alone once more. "What happened here?" She shook her head, trying to clear it, uncertain if she ought to smile or cry. "You planned this? All of this? How—?"

Smiling, Leopold nodded. There was a lightness in his eyes that she had never seen in them before. "I admit, I did," he replied, a bounce in his voice . "As I said before, I heard you. I heard what you said, and I found a way to help us both, to make us both happy."

More than anything, Maryann wanted to believe him. "But my parents, they—"

"I spoke to them," Leopold replied, startling her. "After the way you spoke about them, I could not help but think that they reminded me of my own parents. I love them dearly, and whenever I need them, they stand at my side, never hesitating to offer their full support."

Tears shot to Maryann's eyes. "Mine are exactly like that."

Lifting a hand, Leopold gently brushed a tear from her cheek. "I gathered as much," he whispered. "And that is why I went to see them. I told them everything, and together, we found a solution to your family's financial problems."

Maryann's gaze widened in shock. "You did...? You..." She stilled, then frowned. "Everything? You told them everything?"

Leopold chuckled, then nodded.

"Everything? Even how we—"

"Even how we met," he finished for her, easy laughter now spilling from his lips. "I admit, they turned quite pale, hearing of your nightly escapades." Again, he chuckled, a teasing note coming to his voice, one Maryann had greatly missed with all the seriousness as of late. "But in the end, they understood. They looked at one another, and in that moment, they reminded me of my own parents more than ever before." He pulled her closer, his smile growing more dazzling. "I asked for their blessing, and they gave it."

Maryann stilled, staring up at him, unable to believe her ears. "Are you saying—?"

Leopold grinned from ear to ear. "Yes," he stated, knowing exactly what she was asking. He inhaled a deep breath as though needing to gather his courage. Then he took a step back, his hands grasping hers, holding them tightly and safely. His brown gaze sought hers, and then he said, "Will you marry me?"

It was a simple question, four simple words, and yet, they changed everything.

A cry of joy flew from Maryann's lips, and without thought, she flung herself into his arms. "Yes! Yes, I will marry you."

Laughing with joy, Leopold pulled her deeper into his embrace and then spun her around in circle after circle. Maryann began to feel dizzy before he finally set her back down onto her feet. She gazed up at him, disbelief still clouding her mind. Was he truly hers now? Or rather would he be? As soon as they could whisper their "I do's"?

A thousand thoughts raced through her head, but they were all instantly silenced when Leopold pulled her back into his arms and kissed her as he never had before.

Maryann allowed herself to sink into his embrace, holding nothing back, giving as much as she was taking. And finally, there was no regret, no worry for the future, nothing that could dampen her joy, her bliss, her happiness. How unexpectedly wonderful the days ahead suddenly seemed!

Epilogue

A fortnight later

Elmridge was a beautiful estate full of life and laughter. It stood tall and proud, memories lingering in every corner and new family found in every room. The gardens were in full bloom, sweet scents drifting through the air on a soft summer's breeze. Tall elms stood in clusters as well as in a long row off to the north, like sentinels guarding the estate. It was beautiful and breath-taking, and the moment Maryann set foot upon it, she felt at home.

Leopold's family quickly became her own. It took no more than a few words and a shared look to understand that they belonged together now. Aside from her own parents, Maryann found William and Theresa to be the kindest people she had ever met. Joy stood on all their faces as they gathered outside to celebrate their wedding.

Rather daring, Leopold pulled her into his arms in front of everybody and gave her a long, thorough kiss. Everybody clapped and cheered, and when he finally released her, Maryann was out of breath, but overjoyed to see her friends and family celebrating with her.

Over the course of the past fortnight, Maryann had not only met Leopold's family but also his closest friends, those who had helped to grant them their happily-ever-after after all. She adored his younger brother Frederick instantly for he had the most welcoming nature, always laughing, always teasing. Oliver and Kenneth were like day and night-one rather reckless and the other utterly responsible-but both charming and kind. The young girl Charlotte was overwhelmingly sweet, and Maryann thanked her from the very bottom of her heart for her clever idea as well as her curious mind. Who knew, what would have happened if Charlotte had not eavesdropped on the men's conversation?

Maryann didn't dare think of it.

"You look incandescently happy," Leonora commented with a bright smile as she came to stand beside her, slipping an arm through Maryann's and drawing her close. "As does your new husband."

Maryann felt herself blush but nodded eagerly. "I am most happy," she replied. "I never thought such joy could be possible." Her gaze shifted from her adoring husband to the dear friend by her side. "Thank you for all you have done. I do not have the words to express my gratitude."

Leonora sighed deeply, a warm smile still upon her face as her gaze darted to the edge of the terrace where her own husband stood, dark and forbidding, a bit of a scowl on his face. "At least one of us," Leonora replied, "ought to find true love in marriage. Would you not agree?"

Maryann could see the effort it took Leonora to appear joyful when in truth she could not help but mourn her own loss. "We cannot know what the future will bring," Maryann said, hoping to bring some comfort to her friend's heart. "Perhaps one day you will find yourself looking at your husband and see a different man. Perhaps love can grow over time." She cast her a warm smile. "Anything is possible; you taught me that, and I thank you for it."

"I pray you're right," Leonora replied with a smile; the look in her eyes, however, suggested that she did not honestly believe so. Perhaps not everyone was granted a second chance after all. Maryann knew that she was one of the few fortunate ones, and she would forever be grateful for that.

Looking across the terrace, Leopold watched his new bride exchange joyous words with her dear parents. All three of them looked utterly happy, and Leopold's heart swelled at the sight of it. Everything had worked out as it ought to have, and now a new life was beginning, one Leopold had never dared dream of, but had deep down always been hoping for.

Footsteps made him turn, and his gaze fell on his oldest friend. "Sebastian, I am most happy to see you here." His gaze narrowed as his eyes swept over his friend's face. "You look rather put out; what happened?"

Sebastian heaved a deep sigh, then shook his head. "It does not matter," he replied, coming to stand next to Leopold, his gaze directed outward at the gardens. "Let's not speak of such gloomy things." He turned his head and smiled at Leopold. "Today's a happy day, and I am overjoyed to see you in such high spirits. I never thought it possible." He glanced over to where Maryann stood with her parents. "She is a rare woman and your perfect match, it would seem."

Unable not to, Leopold smiled, a smile of utter bliss. "That she is," he agreed. "I'm certain, your own perfect match is out there waiting for you to find her." Indeed, perhaps all his friend needed was someone to love, someone who would love him in return.

Sebastian scoffed. "My father has other ideas," he snorted derisively. "He is pushing me to wed a Duke's daughter." He looked up, and his gaze met Leopold's. "He does not care about love. He never has, not for his wife or his children. In fact, his life is one most sad, and I would pity him if he did not always force his will upon us." Hanging his head, he snorted, "It would certainly serve him right if I were to marry...say, a baker's daughter." He chuckled darkly.

Leopold heaved a deep sigh, concern for his friend dampening his mood. "I understand your motivation and your anger," he stated empathetically. "But I must urge you not to marry for the wrong reasons. Do not choose a wife based on your father's urgings, but neither choose one in order to spite him. Either choice will only serve to make you unhappy," he clasped a companionable hand upon his friend's shoulder, "and you deserve better whether you believe it or not. I know it to be true."

Meeting Leopold's gaze, Sebastian nodded. "I see the merit of your words," he replied, "but I cannot deny that spiting my father's wishes is a very tempting thought."

Deep concern for his friend settled upon Leopold's heart.

Sebastian sighed, "I can see that my presence here today is the very opposite of beneficial." He stood up tall and turned toward Leopold. "I came to congratulate you, and now I have done so. Enjoy today and all the days to come, my friend. I shall see you soon."

Leopold frowned. "You are leaving so soon?"

"It is for the best," Sebastian replied, sweeping his gaze over the cheerful assembly around them. "My dark mood is not fit for company." And he smiled at Leopold, turned and walked away.

Leaning against the balustrade, Leopold watched his friend leave, wondering what it would take for Sebastian to find happiness himself. In his current state, would he even recognize love should he stumble upon it? Leopold could not deny that he was worried for his friend.

"Are you all right?" came Charlotte's soft voice as she stepped up next to him. She looked so young, full of life and hope, looking at the world and seeing a beautiful place. Her hazel eyes were bright, and her smile genuine.

Turning to look at the young girl, Leopold cast her a warm smile. "I am," he assured her, then glanced across the terrace once more, his eyes settling on Maryann. Instantly, his heart warmed, chasing away the looming clouds Sebastian's words had left behind. "I am very much alright indeed."

She returned his smile. "I am glad to hear it." Then a slight frown came to her face, and she turned her head to look toward the French doors leading inside. "Your friend seemed troubled though," she remarked, ever observant.

Leopold nodded. "He is," he admitted, wondering what else to say. He did not wish to shock Charlotte with the truth, but neither did he want to betray his friend's confidence. "Life is not always easy," he told her, trying his best to put a cheerful note into his voice. "But dear friends make all the difference." He smiled at her warmly.

Blushing slightly, Charlotte briefly averted her gaze. "I'm glad I was able to help." She turned to look at Maryann, who was at this very moment winding her way through the crowd, her bright eyes locked upon his. "You look so very happy together."

"We are," Leopold said enthusiastically, reaching out an arm and pulling a laughing Maryann into a deep embrace. "We are most happy, are we not?"

Maryann smiled up at him. "We most certainly are and ever shall be."

Leopold sighed, wishing all the world could be as happy as they were. Indeed, they were among the most fortunate ones, and he would forever be grateful for that.

THE END

This was the prequel to my USA Today bestselling *Love's Second Chance Series: Tales of Damsels & Knights*.

LOVE'S SECOND CHANCE: TALES OF DAMSELS & KNIGHTS

Are you eager to find out what happens to Frederick and his friends in the future? Do you want to see them fall in love? And what about Charlotte and Leopold's friend Sebastian?

Continue with Frederick's & Ellie's story in **Despised & Desired - The Marquess' Passionate Wife**.

After suffering a tragedy, Ellie suddenly finds herself married to Frederick, a man she's loved almost all her life. Will Ellie be able to claim his heart?

. . .

In case you've read all books of the *Tales of Damsels & Knights*, check out the first installment of the *Highland Tales:* **Tamed & Unleashed - The Highlander's Vivacious Wife**.

After waking up in a strange bed with no memory, Claudia Davenport flees — only to later discover she's pregnant. When her son is kidnapped, she sets out to find him and joins forces with handsome Highlander Garrett MacDrummond, who seems very familiar...

Read a Sneak-Peek

Tamed & Unleashed
The Highlander's Vivacious Wife
(#1 Highland Tales)

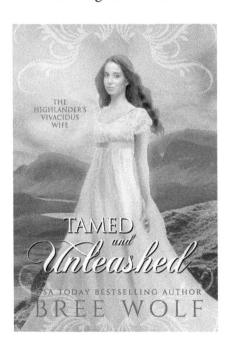

Prologue

Gretna Green, Scotland, Summer 1808 (or a variation thereof)

Upon waking, Claudia Davenport, sister to Viscount Ashwood, found her head throbbing with such intensity that she feared it would split in two. Groaning, she rolled onto her side, her hands reaching up to cover her face in a futile attempt to shield her from the blinding sun penetrating even her closed lids. Had the world gone mad?

Never in her life had Claudia awoken to such pain. Never had the sun been her enemy. Never had she felt sick to her stomach.

Not quite like this.

Pinching her eyes shut, Claudia buried her face in the pillow, slowly forcing one deep breath after another down her throat and into her lungs. To her relief, she found that holding her head still eased the pain somewhat, and so she simply lay there for a long while, breathing in and out.

After a small eternity, her ears began to pick up on various sounds drifting in through the closed windows as well as the door to her room. The sounds of people going about their business. And yet, the sounds were not quite as she remembered them.

As they ought to be.

Something was different, and a frown emerged on her face.

Slowly, she cracked open an eye and peered at her surroundings.

A moment later, Claudia bolted upright in bed.

Instantly, her head rebelled at such treatment, sending jolts of pain through her being that would have brought her to her knees had she been standing. Her hands flew up, pressing hard onto her temples in the hopes of easing the pain. Still, it took a long while before she dared open her eyes again.

Squinting, Claudia took in the small chamber, the simple and sparse furnishings, the lack of luxury. "What happened?" she whispered to herself. "Where am I?"

For this was definitely not her bedchamber back at Farnworth Manor.

This was a room she had never seen before.

Swallowing the panic that began to rise, Claudia closed her eyes once more, trying to remember how on earth she had ended up in this place. The last thing she could recall was attending Lord Campton's ball.

Once more, she heard the soft notes of the music drifting through the large rooms. Again, she found herself standing with the other young debutantes, eyes gliding over the gentlemen in attendance until-

"William," Claudia gasped as his face took form before her inner eye. "We danced. We laughed. We-" Again, a gasp tore from her throat, and one hand fell from her temple covering her mouth in shock. "We ran off."

Trying to swallow the lump in her throat, Claudia once more glanced about the room as though William might have been hiding somewhere in plain sight all along. But he was not. She was alone.

Careful not to move too much, Claudia inhaled a few deep breaths, allowing her mind to wander back to the night before. Slowly, images returned of her taking William's hand and following him outside into the dark night. She remembered him helping her into his carriage, the way he had held her in his arms as the horses had pulled them toward their destination, his assurances that all would be well.

"We eloped," Claudia mumbled, her eyes drifting around the room. "This is...this is an inn...in Gretna Green. It must be." The breath caught in her throat, and she slowly turned her head to the left, her eyes focusing on the other side of the bed.

It was empty, and yet, someone had lain there. There was an unmistakable indentation, and...a warmth lingered that sent a shiver down her back. "What have I done?" Slowly, she pulled back the thin blanket and her heart slammed to a momentary halt.

In the bright morning sun, a few droplets of blood shone on the white linen like rubies.

The air rushed from Claudia's lungs, and the nausea in her stomach sent her flying from the bed. Her body tensed, revolted, and she sank to her knees, one arm reaching for the chamber pot. Then her insides contracted expelling last night's dinner-and drink! -into the small bowl.

When it was over, she sank down, head resting against the side of the bed, her mind momentarily focused on drawing fresh air into her body. Her hand pushed the chamber pot away as the stench of its contents threatened to overwhelm her delicate hold on her body once more.

In her weakened state, Claudia felt numb and strangely detached. Her mind moved slowly as though it did not have the strength to provide her with what she sought: answers.

Still, despite an almost desperate desire to curl up into a ball and hide in a corner, Claudia knew that she could not pretend this had not happened - whatever *this* was!

Had she married William? Had they arrived in Gretna Green, sought out an anvil priest and-?

Claudia froze as an image drifted to the front of her mind, an image of William hanging his head in defeat, his eyes downcast and apologetic...as he had stepped away from her...and followed his elder brother, Viscount Crowemore, to their waiting carriage.

Again, panic welled up as her memories cleared.

Yes, they had come to Gretna Green, but they had not gotten married. William's brother had found them first, ending their adventure by ordering his brother to return with him.

And William had complied.

He had bowed his head.

He had left her.

Shocked beyond words, Claudia stared across the room at the plain wall, reliving the moment disillusionment had set in. She remembered her feeling of betrayal when William had abandoned her, complying with his family's wishes and a long-standing contract. He was to marry a duke's daughter.

Not her.

Despite his promises, he had abandoned her.

Left her behind in Gretna Green.

Alone.

A distant part of Claudia's mind tried to remind her that she had refused to accompany them back to England, cursing and yelling at the top of her voice. However, that part was soon shushed by the sense of betrayal and disappointment that washed over her.

Closing her eyes, Claudia wept for a dream ruined, for a life that was not to be, for the harshness of the world. Still, her emotional turmoil only managed to keep her mind silenced for a short while. Before long, it piped up once more, asking questions Claudia now feared to know the answer to.

If William had indeed returned to England with his brother, then who had slept beside her? Who had spent the night in her room? In her bed? Who had she been intimate with? A complete stranger?

It had to be, for what other answer could there be?

Gritting her teeth, Claudia pushed to her feet, doing her best to ignore the throbbing pain behind her temples as well as the slight swaying of the room. She glimpsed her clothes hanging over the back of a chair and slowly hobbled toward them.

Dressing proved to be quite a challenge in her state, and yet, it provided a momentary relief from the panic that threatened to consume her. Once that was taken care of though, her thoughts immediately refocused on that which she did not know.

And panic returned.

"No!" Claudia snapped, forcing herself not to succumb to this line of thinking for it would lead her nowhere.

What was to be done? Now *that* was a productive question. A question that needed an answer. Here and now.

"I need to get home," Claudia said, feeling her mind clearing as she spoke. "I need to get back." For no matter how angry her brother would be once he learnt what she had done, he would never turn from her. He could be a cold-hearted and unfeeling bastard, but he would not forget his obligation to her, his duty to see to his family.

Of that she was certain.

How to get home, on the other hand, was a different matter. After all, they had come here in William's carriage, and as far as Claudia was aware, she did not have any money on her.

A frown drew down her brows, sending fresh pain through her head. How had she paid for the room? Or had-?

Loud footsteps echoed up the stairs outside her chamber, and Claudia froze. Her eyes were fixed on the door, and her mind was reeling with the thought that she was about to come face to face with whomever she had shared her bed with last night. Would she remember him? Or would he still be a stranger?

The echo grew louder as the man stormed down the corridor...and stopped outside her door.

Inhaling a deep breath, Claudia braced herself for what was to come when the door finally swung open...and her brother stormed in.

Seeing his face, Claudia almost sank to the floor as the air rushed from her lungs. Utter relief filled her, but only at first for the dark look on her brother's face would have sent anyone running for the hills.

For a long moment, they merely looked at one another, speechless. Claudia could see the tension holding him rigid, the way his chest rose and fell as he tried his best to contain his anger, his outrage...his disappointment.

Her brother was not prone to losing his temper-never had been-but the quiet darkness that rested in his eyes sent chills down her back.

"What have you done?" he finally asked, his voice low and menacing as his silver eyes took in the room, the bed, her dishevelled state, the implications that hung in the air. "What were you thinking?"

Claudia felt her chin begin to quiver and tears sting the back of her eyes, and yet, she would not give him the satisfaction of seeing her defeated. Raising her chin, she met his eyes. "It was my choice, not yours. You have no right-"

"That it was," he interrupted, raking a hand through his hair. In two large strides, he was in front of her, his hands gripping her by the upper arms. "This is without a doubt the most foolish thing you've ever done, and whether you like it or not, this time you'll have to pay for it."

Claudia gritted her teeth against the pain thudding behind her temples. "What did you expect when you all but locked me away? I am not free to do anything I want. I-"

"Don't blame me for your mistakes!" he hissed before he stepped back and held the door open for her. "We shall discuss everything further at home."

"If you insist," Claudia snapped, relieved to at least have an answer delivered to her with regard to how she was to get home. Glaring at her brother, she stomped past him, along the corridor and down the stairs, all the while berating him, doing her best to ignore the pounding in her head.

"Be quiet!" he hissed once they'd reached the taproom. His eyes took in the many travellers coming and going before he took her by the arm and all but dragged her outside.

Despite digging in her heels, Claudia had no hope of delaying him. "You're the most awful brother in all of England," she retorted, wondering why on earth she was blaming him. And yet, she could not stop. She was not yet ready to face the mess she had made, and at present, he was the only one she could blame.

It was a distraction-nothing more-and one day she would have to face reality.

But tomorrow was soon enough.

Never would she have expected for the one adventure she had ever dared to embark upon to end in this way.

Never.

Series Overview

LOVE'S SECOND CHANCE: TALES OF LORDS & LADIES

LOVE'S SECOND CHANCE: TALES OF DAMSELS & KNIGHTS

LOVE'S SECOND CHANCE: HIGHLAND TALES

THE WHICKERTONS IN LOVE

FORBIDDEN LOVE SERIES

HAPPY EVER REGENCY SERIES

For more information visit www.breewolf.com

About Bree

USA Today bestselling and award-winning author, Bree Wolf has always been a language enthusiast (though not a grammarian!) and is rarely found without a book in her hand or her fingers glued to a keyboard. Trying to find her way, she has taught English as a second language, traveled abroad and worked at a translation agency as well as a law firm in Ireland. She also spent loooong years obtaining a BA in English and Education and an MA in Specialized Translation while wishing she could simply be a writer. Although there is nothing simple about being a writer, her dreams have finally come true.

"A big thanks to my fairy godmother!"

Currently, Bree has found her new home in the historical romance genre, writing Regency novels and novellas. Enjoying the mix of fact and fiction, she occasionally feels like a puppet master (or mistress? Although that sounds weird!), forcing her characters into ever-new situations that will put their strength, their beliefs, their love to the test, hoping that in the end they will triumph and get the happily-ever-after we are all looking for.

If you're an avid reader, sign up for Bree's newsletter on **www. breewolf.com** as she has the tendency to simply give books away. Find out about freebies, giveaways as well as occasional advance reader copies and read before the book is even on the shelves!

Connect with Bree and stay up-to-date on new releases:

facebook.com/breewolf.novels

twitter.com/breewolf_author

instagram.com/breewolf_author

bookbub.com/authors/bree-wolf

amazon.com/Bree-Wolf/e/B00FJX27Z4